UNSEELIE

TIES

Book Fourteen of the Hayle Coven Novels

PATTI LARSEN

ALSO BY
PATTI LARSEN

The Hayle Coven Universe

The Hunted Series
Fiona Fleming Cozy Mysteries
The Nightshade Cases
The Clone Chronicles
The Diamond City Trilogy
Didi and the Gunslinger

and much, much more.
Find your new favorite author at
pattilarsen.com
Sign up for new releases
bit.ly/pattilarsenemail

chapter one

Class bored me. Mostly. How could I possibly take interest in the chain reaction of fire, water, earth and air through tiny little samples on a glass slate when I'd flown with dragons, fought demons and evil witches, battled vampire queens, and almost died doing it? I sighed, chin on my fist as my lab partner, Tippy Meeks, prodded the small clump of dirt to start the show.

"Observe," Mr. Howermall, my Elemental Interactions teacher said in his low, dull voice devoid of anything resembling excitement or enthusiasm. Tippy tossed her thick red hair over one shoulder and crossed her eyes at me. She was the only saving grace in this entire stupid class. "Earth and water are in opposition."

Right. I was supposed to be watching as Tippy's magic nudged the hovering droplet of water over the loose soil, scattering it. Wow. How awesome was that?

1

Sarcasm, my best friend.

One week into my second year of witch's college and here I was wishing something really awful would happen just so I'd have an excuse to get out of this boring class.

Tippy winked and fluttered her fingers over the mess she'd made. A little clay man rose from the mix, dancing a jig on the glass while giving Mr. Howermall the finger.

Oh my, yes. Much, much better.

I pressed both hands over my mouth to stifle my giggling and made a fake angry face at Tippy who let the tiny mud man collapse.

Seriously. This was basic stuff, for babies. Okay, okay, so I hadn't exactly been the best student growing up, but if this was all we learned in college, I was so ready to call it a day and head for home.

"Now," Mr. Howermall said, "introduce air to your experiment."

I gestured at Tippy as she raised one hand. My turn. Mr. Howermall wanted air in there, huh? I could handle that. A tiny tornado danced its way into life, complete with a softly echoing howl. Tippy raised her mud man again and we both nearly collapsed into laughter as the twister lifted him up and spun him like a top. Bits of mud flew out of the tornado to splatter Tippy's shirt. Still giggling, I raised a shield to protect us, too late. She brushed her hand over the tight white t-shirt she wore, the mud falling to the counter. "Bite Me" glared back from the pair of ruby lips balanced on her impressive cleavage.

Her voluptuousness always made me wonder if I could do a little enhancement of my own. Not that I was flat or anything, but I felt more than inadequate when I stood next to her.

Then again, I didn't have guys staring at my chest instead of in my eyes. Not that Tippy minded. Thus the t-shirt.

"Excellent." Mr. Howermall didn't even leave his desk to observe us, instead leaning his rounded belly against the back of his chair, face as disinterested as his voice. "Next, apply fire to the other three and record your findings."

If I didn't get to do something challenging soon, I was going to lose my mind. All of the things that happened to me over the last three years or so left me a little jaded. Okay, more than a little. I leaned back, my good humor fading, and let Tippy introduce fire into the tornado. Mud man shook, expanded and then exploded outward, splattering the inside of the shield with his clayness.

"Ew." Tippy's eyes glittered with wickedness. "Let's do that again."

I laughed softly, keeping my head down, though I was now firmly convinced Mr. Howermall wouldn't have left his desk or noticed we were up to no good even if his ass was on fire. "Thanks, but no thanks."

"You're no fun," she pouted, her wide, full lips pulling down, glowing with lip gloss. And then she smiled and prodded me. "Just kidding," she said. "This is lame."

"Really?" I glared at Mr. Howermall. "I hadn't noticed."

Sashenka Hensley, my roommate and bestie, turned around from two desks up to roll her eyes at me. I would have chosen her for a lab partner in a second, if Mr. Howermall hadn't assigned us. At least I had Tippy. Poor Shenka was stuck with Richard Neuman, a Santos witch. I didn't have anything against him, per se, but he was the clumsiest guy with magic I'd ever met. After being stuck beside him in Mixed Magicks lab last semester dodging flying power, I felt Shenka's pain, but didn't love her enough to trade places.

She had to learn life sucked sometimes.

Snort.

I watched her carefully handle her klutzy partner and my mind went to our conversation from the summer. Shenka's desire to leave her coven led me to talk to her about being my second, something she'd seemed excited about when she mentioned it again at Sunny and Uncle Frank's wedding. But every time I brought it up since starting back to school, she made an excuse or changed the subject.

She changed her mind, was my only guess. And as

much as I wanted her to be my second, needed one thanks to Gram's prodding, and knew Shenka was the perfect choice, I understood her reluctance. Her older sister, Tallah, was my friend, one of the only younger witches leading covens that I knew. The last thing I wanted was to make enemies of the Hensley coven by stealing Shenka away. But if she wasn't happy, it had to be detrimental to the family.

Still, I understood. But it made me feel sad and a little frustrated.

"You've been sighing all class," Tippy whispered as she swept the mess from table with air magic and into the trash. "Either tell me what's up or stop breathing." She winked once, twining a lock of red curls around her finger.

"Things don't always work out the way you want them, I guess." I shrugged. "My grandmother's been pushing me to recruit a second so she can hand off the rest of the family power."

I might as well have told Tippy her favorite rock band stood right behind her. Green eyes lit up and widened, one hand grasping mine, her perfectly manicured and very sharp nails digging into my wrist as she leaned close with a smile growing across her face. I understood my mistake almost immediately.

"Syd," Tippy said, voice quivering with emotion, "I would love. Yes. Love. To audition to be your second.

LOVE." She bounced on her stool, still clinging to me. "I've been wanting to leave my family and make my own mark. And your coven..." she whistled softly before sobering a little. "I know you can't just choose me," she said. "That we'll have to talk about it. But," she grabbed me again, grin as big as ever, "I'd be honored if you'd let me try out."

Like she was applying to be a cheerleader.

Oh boy.

Before I could say anything, a deep, echoing chime rang. Mr. Howermall sighed and actually looked relieved himself. "Dismissed."

I rose and moved to the softly opening door, Tippy chattering away beside me while I inwardly cringed at the thought of having her as my second. I adored her, of course I did. She was one of the few friends I chose to have who didn't judge me or treat me differently. Unlike most of the rest of the student body who were either afraid of me or hated my guts for varying reasons having to do with family attachments.

I let Tippy talk, retreating as I considered the problem. While I wouldn't likely choose her, I knew I did have to make a decision. Any idea of doing what Tallah did and picking my own sister was out of the question. Not only was Meira more demon than I was on the outside, forced to hide her red skin and black horns, not to mention her glowing amber eyes behind a facade of humanity, she and I weren't really on talking terms at the moment.

Ever since her return from Demonicon, Meira was different, darker and more on edge. I hardly blamed her for the change. She'd been purposely hooked on nectar by Sassafras's evil mother, Sekaniphestat, used by Ameline to track and try to stop me from blocking Ameline's way to the Node keeping Demonicon together. And I hadn't been there for Meira, to protect her. To keep her safe.

Guilt, thy name is Syd.

But even if she forgave me and didn't act distant and cold when I managed to track her down, she was now heir to the Second Seat of Demonicon. That position trumped the coven.

My heart hurt thinking about my little sister. Now aged beyond her normal eleven-year old appearance thanks to the nectar, Mom decided sending her off to a different school for the year would be a good change for her. Which meant sending Meira to Europe, living with Council Leader Applegate. Yes, I could have reached her at any point, even ridden the veil across territories to visit. But she'd made it pretty clear when we'd parted just before I came to Harvard she needed space.

Namely, by closing me out completely.

I took the hint and the hit to my guilt and let her go.

Even worse, my ever-present support system, my

silver Persian demon boy Sassafras, was on Demonicon for the next few weeks. An invitation to help Dad and my grandfather solidify their new rule wasn't something he could turn down. As much as I knew it was a huge honor and Sass was excited to go, I missed him every single day.

He deserved a life. Of course he did. I just wished he could live it around me at the moment.

I caught Shenka's eye as we cleared the exit to Coven Hall and passed through to the library on our way to lunch. She smiled, slowed to wait for me, even as my gaze drifted past her to a girl with long, black hair.

Ameline. No, of course not. The girl turned to smile at her companion, showing me her profile. Not my nemesis. And yet, the reminder was a jab to my guts and, I knew, the source of my discontent with attending college.

What did school matter when I should be out there hunting down Ameline Benoit?

And killing her.

chapter two

Bloodthirsty thoughts aside, I slid into a seat at our favorite table beside Liam, who beamed up at me, half-rising as I joined him. My handsome Sidhe friend leaned in to hug me with one arm while Tippy took the seat next to him. I felt him tense the moment she did, how his arm fell away, the sparkling green in his hazel eyes fading. His head dropped, strawberry blonde hair falling over his face as Tippy leaned up against him with a broad wink.

"Thanks for saving us seats, handsome."

Okay, she was never, ever, ever going to be my second. And if she didn't stop pressing her gigantic rack against his arm I was going to tear her a new one.

Temper, temper, Syd.

Shut up, conscience.

Fortunately, there was enough room I slid over a little, allowing Liam to pull away from the aggressive redhead while I clenched my teeth against my unwarranted jealousy. How many times had I told Liam we couldn't be together? And yet, I still went a little—okay a lot—crazy when Tippy hit on him.

Who had the real problem, then?

Good thing we weren't alone. Sashenka sank down beside me as my bodywere, Charlotte, hovered behind. There were times I almost forgot she was around these days. Not because she disappeared on me or anything. Quite the opposite. But since my second—and then third—trip to Demonicon, Charlotte had become colder, more detached, and I knew my absence hurt her feelings as well as her physiology. Thanks to the link she'd created between us, some kind of ridiculous ritualistic honor bond, she suffered if I wasn't with her 24/7. Like it was my fault. We'd had to tie her down when I went back to Demonicon for my demon grandmother's funeral.

She hadn't forgiven me since then. In fact, she'd dyed her long, blonde hair jet black and taken to wearing a lot of eyeliner and mascara. I seemed to recall she was a redhead like Tippy when we met, but when I asked Charlotte about it, she simply shrugged. "So I like to color my hair," she snapped, sullen and sulky.

I hadn't responded past a meeped, "It looks really nice," leaving it at that.

I wished she'd just sit with us. She made my life even more uncomfortable when she hovered like she did.

Made me feel really visible. As in, oh look, there's the puffed up princess, Sydlynn Hayle, who thinks she's so special she has a bodyguard.

Sigh.

I dissected my sandwich with twitching fingers, feeling a little sorry for myself, when Tippy went and opened her big mouth.

"Have you all heard Syd's news?" She practically gushed she was so excited. I didn't get the chance to shush her up before she blurted it out. "She's looking for a second. And I'm in the running."

Hey, hang on a minute. I opened my mouth to shut her down, only to catch the hurt in Shenka's eyes. My bestie turned away while the other girls all oohed and aahed.

"I'd test for it," Nicci Mortimer said, dirty blonde hair bouncing in her high pigtails as she sipped a soda, "but I know I don't have the power you need, Syd."

My empathy kicked in immediately. "That's not true, Nicci."

"I'm planning to teach," Josie Ambrose said, pale skin almost glowing in the light from the stained glass windows, her hair as black as Charlotte's, "or I'd be all over that."

"You can't have her." Tippy reached across Liam and grasped my hand.

"I don't know," Donalda Pierce said in her slow

drawl, tall, thin body leaning forward, wide gray eyes sparkling with humor as she teased our friend. "Maybe I'd like to give it a go, Syd."

Though they were all part of Shenka's family coven, I'd be much more inclined to choose this quiet, powerful Hensley witch than her red haired counterpart and actually paused to consider. Even as my heart churned over the look on Shenka's face.

"Excuse me," she whispered, rising from the table, taking her tray with her. She left us, head down, dumping her uneaten lunch in the trash while I struggled with what to do.

Sheesh. She was the one who didn't want to talk about it.

I was about to go after her when I felt Mom touch my mind. *Syd, sweetheart, can you come to my office?* She sounded a little tense, hidden behind her Momness. No one else would have noticed, probably. But I knew her very well and felt my stomach tighten in response.

Anything I should have forewarning about? I rose with a wave to the others, a squeeze to Liam's shoulder and a mouthed, "Mom," so they knew where I was going before turning and heading for the exit.

Just come, please. She sighed mentally.

I am, I sent as I descended the steps of Annenberg Hall and crossed the street to the Yard. *But you sound stressed so I thought I'd ask.*

Her hesitation told me everything I needed to know. *I'll fill you in when you get here*, she sent before cutting me off very firmly.

How lovely.

Charlotte paced silently behind me as I crossed the grassy Yard, backpack over one shoulder, my feet heavier with each step as I considered the numerous disasters Mom could be shielding me from. By the time I passed through the front door of Massachusetts Hall where she kept her office and climbed onto the elevator, I was so worked up I was sweating.

I often wonder why you allow yourself to become concerned with something of which you don't know the details. My vampire's gentle voice calmed me immediately before sparking a bit of temper.

You know my life, I sent back as the elevator doors dinged.

Our life, she corrected softly.

Whatever. *You should be nervous too*, I sent. *Why aren't you?*

She paused. Sighed. *When you put it that way.*

That broke my nerves and made me laugh.

I thought this wasn't funny? She sounded so confused I giggled harder.

I love you, I sent. *But sarcasm isn't your forte.*

She fell silent as I grinned out the last of my tension and walked through the large wooden door into Mom's sitting room.

The parlor was all dark wood, from floor to walls to ceiling and though the height soared above me, I always felt like I was in a cave. The glaring faces of the previous Council Leaders in portraits lining the walls didn't make things any better.

The place gave me the creeps.

Maurice waited for me, his little mustache quivering. My mother's secretary and I didn't get along very well. Partly because he was a pompous snob and a toad. His old-fashioned waistcoat always hugged his very round belly and reminded me of a fat frog.

"Coven Leader," he sniffed as though I didn't deserve the title, "please leave your dog at the door."

Oh *hell* no. Charlotte had been a bone of contention between us before, but this was the first time he openly insulted her. The only thing saving his nasty little life? Mom entered the room at the exact same moment he insulted my bodywere.

Then again, from the scowl on her face, he'd gone from my rock and into Mom's hard place.

"Maurice." She snapped his name. He jumped as he turned to face her, so comical I almost laughed. Would have if I wasn't pissed off. "You may go."

"Council Leader." He spluttered a moment. "The meeting."

"I told you to leave." Mom was usually really good at

hiding her anger. But I could tell she'd taken personal offence to his insult. Either that or whoever waiting in her office had already stirred her anger and she was just taking it out on a convenient target.

Didn't bode well for him either way.

"While you're gone," Mom's words cut the air, "reconsider your tone and your attitude toward my daughter and her companion. Carefully."

Maurice's shock seemed so genuine I had to shake my head.

"Council Leader," he said. "I am your personal secretary."

"Are," she said. "At the moment. But these things can change. Now go."

He seemed to deflate, paling, hands fluttering before him. Mom stared him down, arms crossed over her chest, cold and imposing until he turned with a small cry and rushed past me, eyes full of tears. I almost applauded. Almost.

So close.

Mom sighed when he left, dropping her firm stance, sadness on her face as she came forward and took Charlotte's hands. "Forgive him," she said. "He's a fool. I would have fired him long ago if he weren't so good at his job."

Charlotte's eyes widened, cheeks very pink as she bowed to Mom. "It's no matter," she mumbled, clearly touched by Mom's defense of her.

What had she gone through in her life she didn't expect her friends to stand up for her?

Oh, right. She was raised with the Dumonts who treated her worse than Maurice ever could.

I squeezed Charlotte's hand, keeping a hold on her as I faced Mom. "Thanks."

She shook her head. "I've looked past many things," she said. "But there is only so much I will tolerate." Mom's blue eyes darkened before she grimaced, shoulders setting.

So I'd guessed right. Bad news behind door number one had been the basis for her temper. Whatever she was about to tell me, I wasn't going to like it very much.

"Just spit it out," I said. "You know I'll blow up and then we'll deal with it."

Mom laughed softly before kissing my cheek. "Syd," she said. "I love you."

"Yeah, yeah," I said, "I love you too. Now dump it."

She nodded once, face set. "We've taken on a special lecturer this semester," she said. "I just wanted to warn you before you met him again."

Okay. "Who is it?" I ran through the various jerktards I'd met over the last few years, stomach knotting.

Mom hesitated. "You must understand," she rushed out, "he might have issues with his own people, but he's never been accused of wrong doing against witches." She winced. "Not officially."

This had to be very bad or Mom wouldn't be soft shoeing her way around me.

"Mom," I said.

"I'm sorry, Syd," she said. "I'm under a great deal of pressure to accept him." Her eyes pleaded with me. "Don't freak out. Promise me."

"No promises," I said, whole body tense, Charlotte's too, from the grip I still had on her hand.

Mom turned and headed for her office, gesturing for me to join her. "It's a complicated and delicate situation," she said, lowering her voice as her hand settled on the doorknob. "Do you understand?"

I sighed, forcing myself to relax before nodding. "Okay fine," I whispered as I crowded behind her, not sure I wanted to uncover her mystery guest or not. "No freaking out. But I might swear."

Mom was already opening the door and striding inside, so I wasn't sure if she heard me. My eyes swept the large room, over the three leather chairs before her desk, the matching three gray heads turning to smile at me. But it was the tall, silver haired man with the green eyes and silky smile who brought me up short with a gasp.

Mom needn't have worried I'd freak. I was too shocked, numb and breathless while Shaylee screeched in fury.

"Your Highness," Hall Venner said, the Sidhe

Unseelie Lord Venemeth bowing at the waist. "It's a pleasure to see you again."

chapter three

It didn't take me long to go from stunned silence to fury. Okay, so Mom was right to worry. So. Right. The last time I'd seen the back end of Venner he'd been trying to kill me. Had almost killed Liam's grandfather, Fergus, forcing us to send the old Gatekeeper through the Gate so the seal could be rebuilt after we failed to answer the knock.

All so whiny fairy boy here could run home to his Sidhe momma or something equally pathetic.

Before I could gather myself enough to ask what the bloody hell was going on, a small, slender witch of advanced age stood from the leather chair she'd claimed in front of Mom's desk and smiled at me. Well, kind of smiled. More like barracuda'd. I'd never seen that many teeth in someone's mouth before.

"Welcome, Coven Leader," she said in a voice so

graveled I was amazed she could speak. "It's a delight to finally meet you."

"Sydlynn," Mom rushed into the conversation with a forced smile of her own and tension in every line of her body, "may I introduce Gertrude Santos, the head of our school's board of governors."

So that was the way things were, huh? The other two women, equally as ancient, turned to face me though neither bothered to get up. Tall and lanky hunched into her seat on one side, almost Gertrude's height even sitting, while portly and round, with tiny glasses she couldn't possibly see a thing out of, perched on the other, sausage fingers picking at her lower lip over and over.

"This is Elegance Faster," Mom gestured to giant witch. Elegance? Holy. Her mom had a terrible sense of humor. "And Periwinkle Rhodes." Seriously. What was wrong with witches and naming their kids? Every witch mother needed to be taken out and shaken vigorously.

My own included.

I bobbed my head, eyes returning to Venner and his smirk. I hated smirkers. There was just something about the expression that drove me so close to the edge I could barely stand it. And while Quaid was an expert and Ram, my demon friend, could pull off a rather impressive show, Venner had centuries to polish his, elevating his smirk to sparkly shine.

Oh how I would have loved to rub it in the dirt and

see how much stuck.

"Mom," I said, not even trying to play nice. "You do know who this is, don't you?"

Venner actually winked. While smirking.

He was a dead fairy.

Before Mom could answer, Gertrude spoke up, thin hands flapping, tiny nose wrinkled as though she smelled something bad. I knew I did. "Lord Venemeth has been completely up front with us about his reasons for being on our plane," she said, my ears aching from the harshness of her voice.

"No," I said, "I'm pretty sure he hasn't. Because if he told you everything, he wouldn't be standing here right now. Not without chains, anyway." Chains would be a nice touch. I could probably find a way to make some out of the metal in Mom's office.

Gertrude's little face crumpled in anger, beady eyes flickering to Mom and back again. "We are aware of his attempt to overtake the Gate in your territory." Why did it sound like she blamed me for the mess he'd almost made? Oh no she did *not*. "But seeing as his infraction," oh, just a minor mistake almost setting the whole of the Sidhe free in the streets of Wilding Springs, right, gotcha, "had nothing to do with witches," she said what? "there is no cause for retribution."

"What do you think I am?" I had a temper. I was well aware of the fact. And there were times I let it carry me off when perhaps I shouldn't. But standing there with this pompous, arrogant, hideous old witch telling me all was forgiven for no good reason fired up all of my magic parts until my demon roared her rage. Shaylee shuddered in her fury, her fear of Venner long gone. Even my vampire hissed and squirmed inside me, and she hadn't had contact with him at all. I drew a breath to hold back what I wanted to say before going on. "He attacked me, Governor. I'm a witch, remember?"

Elegance cleared her throat, a surprisingly squeaky girl voice emerging from her lips. "You were acting as Princess Shaylee," she said. "And so the attack itself was against the Sidhe, and not other magical beings." She glanced over her shoulder at Venner, smiling at him. "Which we wouldn't be willing to tolerate."

Oh. My. Swearword.

"It's true, Your Highness," Venner said in his smooth voice, stabbing Shaylee with each and every velvet word. "I had no idea who you were when we first met. It was you who revealed your additional powers to me in the Gate room." The bastard. THE BASTARD. "Had I known, I certainly never would have acted the way I did." My mind scrambled over my memories, hating he was right. "And indeed, when I discovered who you were, I left. Did I not?" One crystal green eye winked again, slowly.

Not exactly. But damn it. Close enough.

Damn damn damn damn.

"I've since reformed," Venner said, smile widening as he adjusted his perfectly tailored suit, long, silver hair falling over one shoulder. The three governors nodded with him as he stepped around their chairs toward me while I clenched my hands into fists and tried to keep myself from punching him in the guts. "I know now I will never be able to return to the Unseelie court or my home." So sad. Boo freaking hoo. "And because of that understanding, I've decided to stop fighting my fate and embrace it." He turned to take Gertrude's hand, bending in a fluid bow over her fingers, pressing his wide, full lips to the wrinkled skin while she simpered.

Actually simpered. Shaylee's internal gagging noises almost made me laugh.

Almost.

"Sidhe teachers are so hard to come by," Periwinkle finally spoke up, round cheeks pinking as she focused on Venner. "And Lord Venemeth is so knowledgeable." Yeah. I could just imagine. Gross, ew, thanks for the mental image.

"You're actually going to give a felon," I glared at him, not caring what the ladies thought, frankly, "who has been kicked out of his own realm and committed acts of violence against humans tied to the Sidhe access to young witches? As a teacher?"

They had to be out of their little biddy minds.

Gertrude's face darkened as Periwinkle gasped and Elegance's large, bulging eyes widened further. Mom's hand on my shoulder was the only thing holding me back.

"While I understand your concerns," Mom said, "this meeting is a courtesy." *Please, just trust me, Syd.* "I requested you be told in private," *there's more to this than you know.* "Because of your history with Lord Venemeth." She nodded to Venner. "The decision has already been made. My lord, thank you for joining us. Governors." Mom bowed her head again as the other two witches stood, Elegance towering over her two compatriots while Periwinkle's hips almost knocked over her chair on the way by. "I look forward to attending Lord Venemeth's lectures myself."

They knew a dismissal when they heard it. Gertrude led the way with a harrumph and a glare at me, waving one hand at Mom over her shoulder while Elegance bent carefully, shoulders almost brushing the top of the doorway, Periwinkle linking her arm though Venner's on the way out with an outrageous blown kiss he accepted graciously.

He caught my eye just as he pulled the door closed behind him.

His sparkled.

I spun on Mom the moment we were alone, a million swear words on my lips. "You know this is a really bad idea, right? He has something planned."

Mom sighed and took her chair, gesturing for me to sit. I couldn't, choosing to pace instead, wondering how I was going to tell Liam the Sidhe who most likely murdered his father, almost killed his grandfather and blackmailed his mother was here on campus.

"I know," Mom said.

"That's helpful," I shot back. But at least she agreed with me.

"Syd." Mom fixed me with her blue eyes, power reaching for me. She felt stronger than ever, the full weight of the Council's magic behind her, but she didn't use it to force me to stop. She just let me feel her and know she stood behind me completely.

That pulled me up short to stare at her.

"If you know," I said. "If you're aware he's no good, why are you letting him into the school at all? Why haven't you had the Enforcers arrest his skinny Sidhe ass?"

"Because he has the support of the Council majority," Mom said, so calm and level I actually sank into the first chair, wrapped instantly in the sickening scent of roses Periwinkle wore, sitting forward to avoid it. "And the board of governors. Which makes me wonder how he managed it."

My mom was one smart cookie. My temper cooled a little as I rested my elbows on her desk and my chin in my hands. "So now what? Mom, this is nuts." The thought of

25

him teaching made me want to stand up and pace again.

"Now," she said, "you and I attend his lectures." Sparks of blue magic fell from her fingertips as she gestured to the door, her own anger finally showing. "Between the two of us, we will uncover what he has planned and put an end to it."

I found myself grinning. "How did you get so clever?"

Mom laughed, a deep, rich sound, eyes shining. "I had a good teacher." Her power hugged me. "Now, will you trust me and help me handle this?"

Wow. Her offer was a total first. Which meant there was no way I could turn her down.

"I'm in," I said.

CHAPTER FOUR

The first place I headed after leaving Mom was Liam's dorm. Normally, the Yard housing was only for freshmen. But that was a human rule. For the duration of our stay, witches had our own private floors in each of the brick buildings surrounding the Yard, the same rooms in fact for the entire three years. So I had no trouble tracking back across the grass to Matthew Hall and Liam's room.

He answered my knock with a smile, as always, though his happy expression faded when he saw the look on my face just before I pushed past him and inside. Charlotte stopped outside the door, closing it behind me, giving us privacy. Not that we needed it, but I could only guess the weregirl had no desire to listen to me rant.

Neither did I, for that matter. I clenched a firm hold

27

on myself, swearing I wouldn't go nuts on my sweet Sidhe friend, and spun to face him.

"I just wanted to warn you," I said. Level voice? Check. Temper in control? Check. Plans for murdering Venner? Checkarooni, yes indeedy doodle.

Liam's answering frown held concern for me. "Okay. What happened?" He reached for me, drew me against him, hugging me to his broad chest, one hand stroking my hair while the other tucked against the small of my back. Just being in his arms made me feel better as Shaylee sighed and welcomed the touch of her people's magic. "No matter what it is," Liam said, voice rumbling in my ear, the scent of fabric softener and fresh turned earth all around me, "we can handle it. Right?"

I nodded, hugging him back. "We can," I said. Sighed. Relaxed. He was so right.

Liam leaned away and smiled down at me. "Now hit me," he said. "What's going on?"

My fingers clenched around his t-shirt as I bit my lower lip. "There's a new teacher here this year," I said, struggling with just dumping it on him or easing him into the news.

Liam's brows came together, eyes flickering away from mine as his large body tensed. "Oh?"

A terrible and aching understanding flowered inside me. "Yeah," I said, pulling away from him as Liam ducked his head, sunlight from his window catching the red in his blonde hair. "We both know him."

Liam sighed deeply, shoving his hands in his back pockets, shuffling his feet. "Syd," he said. "I already know Venner is here."

Explosion imminent. "And you were planning on filling me in when?"

His hazel eyes sparked with glints of green as he finally met my gaze. "I didn't know how," he said. "I knew you'd be upset."

He hadn't seen upset. Nope nope. "Well," I snarled, "I just found out in front of the board of governors and my mother. So thanks for the heads up." I'd always considered Quaid a bit of a jerkasaurus. Okay, more than a bit, depending on the circumstances. But Liam? No, not my Liam.

"I'm sorry." He reached for me, but I batted his hands away. "I really am."

Grumble, mumble. "How did you find out?" I was willing to let it go. Fine, whatever. Until he winced and looked away for the second time.

Tell me I wasn't going to have to kick his butt.

"Mom told me." Liam's shoulders slumped as he spoke, hands once again returning to his back pockets.

Second major shockage of the day. "Your *what*?" The last time I'd seen Sonja O'Dane, she'd been whisked off against her will when Venner took her and that hideous, despicable woman, Hortense Spaft, with him when his attempt on the Gate failed.

Ms. Spaft. My old Vice Principal when she wasn't conniving to steal Sidhe power and take control of the Gate. The Mistress of Detention herself.

If she was with Venner, she was toast.

Liam turned from me, sitting on the edge of his bed. "Mom got in touch about two weeks ago," he said. "When you were on Demonicon for the funeral." This was what happened when I left the plane? Really? And why hadn't Galleytrot told me? The giant black hound of the Wild Hunt was supposed to keep an eye on Liam, not let him interact with possible risks. "Don't blame Galleytrot," he said, quashing that particular lecture I'd planned for later. "He doesn't know."

I didn't bother telling Liam it was the stupid dog's job to know. And he'd be about as happy as I was Liam was back in contact with his Unseelie mother.

"Are you crazy?" I wanted to shake him, but he looked so miserable all I could do was stand there and fight the need to shout. "What were you thinking?"

Liam lifted his head, tears in his eyes. "I know you think I'm weak," he whispered. "But no matter what happened, Syd, she's still my mother."

Ack. Okay. Family loyalty I understood, even misguided loyalty. Deep breath, girlfriend. "When were you going to tell me?"

He wiped at his eyes, frowning. I could see his back

straighten, knew I'd pushed him as far as I could. Liam was sweet and gentle, but he had a breaking point and I guessed his mother was at the top of his "do not push" list.

And honestly? I was out of line and I knew it. Jeeze. I really had to do an inventory of my temper if my friend had to use anger in return. Get a grip, Syd.

Liam confirmed what I was thinking. "You've made it pretty clear you don't want to be with me," he said, long arms hugging himself as he half turned away. "So it's none of your business, is it?"

Anger flashed over, but I grasped for my vampire to cool it off. "It is," I said as gently as I could. "Liam, like it or not, neither of us can act with autonomy. We have responsibilities, not just to others, but to this plane. And I'm sorry, but you obviously knew you weren't thinking rationally if you hid this from Galleytrot."

Liam flinched. Yup, right on the money. I hated to prod him, I really did. But damn it, one of us had to be a grown up about it.

"I know," Liam said. "But she's my mom."

"And Venner?" I sat next to Liam, one hand on his knee, letting him feel I wasn't angry any more. Nope, just empathetic. Poor guy.

Liam nodded, releasing his grip on himself, covering my hand with his. "He's a different story," Liam said.

Good to know we were on the same page there, at

least.

"But I won't act against him." Liam's fingers squeezed mine. "Mom asked me not to."

Of course she did. "That's okay," I said. "It's taken care of." Hopefully. As long as Mom was willing to follow through when the time came. Not that I didn't believe she would, but there was enough history of her leaving me to clean up messes she couldn't or wouldn't handle, I wasn't completely comfortable with the situation.

"I'm sorry I didn't tell you," Liam said. "And Galleytrot. I just knew you'd be angry."

I left him a short time later, reaching for the black hound the moment Liam's door closed behind me, Charlotte on my heels. It took a little effort with him behind the wards guarding the Gate cavern, but Shaylee, boosted by my earth magic, helped enough to knock on the shielding and summon the dog to the outside world.

Syd. Galleytrot's mind touched mine, the rumble of a spring thunderstorm in his mental voice. I shivered as I often did when his power touched me, the elemental forces of the Sidhe Wild Hunt running through his magic. *Something's wrong?*

Why do you say that? I paused in the darkening Yard under a spreading tree and leaned against the rough bark, hiding in the growing shadows for some privacy.

Because you only get in touch when there's a problem. He

snorted softly in my head.

Oh. Ouch. I really needed to work on my communication skills. *Well, you're right*, I sent. And filled him in on the afternoon of revelations.

Galleytrot's swearing encompassed several languages and lasted at least a minute before his power calmed, rippling over me as he pulled himself together. *What was he thinking?*

I don't think he was, I sent. *You know his mom is all he has left.*

The hound sighed. *Not a good enough reason*, he grumbled. *And Venemeth? Your mother is playing a dangerous game, Syd.*

Tell me about it. I pushed off from the tree and headed for my dorm, just wanting to collapse on my bed and forget this day even happened.

I'll talk to Liam, Galleytrot sent. *Firmly.*

Don't be too hard on him, I sent. *But keep a mental eye on him, would you?*

I could feel his tension like a growing storm. *I wish I could be there directly.*

Someone has to watch the Gate while Liam is here, I sent. *And you volunteered.* Like we had anyone else to do the job. *You're more valuable there.*

I suppose. I had a mental picture of him shaking his huge head, the Gate behind him before he cut me off from the visual. *Still.*

Just be vigilant, I sent. *Who knows what Venner is really up to?*

I will. Galleytrot sent me a rush of power, the rumble of an earthquake. *Watch him. Both hims. And if you see Sonja... Liam is too important to risk, Syd.*

You don't have to convince me. I paused at the bottom of the stairs to my dorm. With a quick hug, I let him go, hoping I was just being paranoid.

Yeah, right. Because nothing bad ever happened to the people I loved.

CHAPTER FIVE

Charlotte hissed softly at me as I mounted the last step and headed down the hall to my room. I was lost in thought, head down. Good thing one of us paid attention. Her hand on my arm, pulling me back as she eased around me, brought my head up as Charlotte put herself between me and the woman standing outside my door.

Sonja O'Dane met my gaze over Charlotte's shoulder, her hands clutching reflexively at the strap of her shoulder bag as she pushed off from where she leaned against the wall. I approached slowly, gesturing for Charlotte to stand down. My wereguard grunted softly, sniffing the air, but allowed me to gain the lead again, though I knew how fast she could react if Sonja meant me harm.

I almost hoped she did. It would be awesome to see

35

Charlotte take the woman down.

Syd. Be nice. Liam's mom.

Grrr.

Sonja seemed hesitant, almost apologetic, as I finally reached her. She fidgeted, manicured nails scraping over the leather strap of her purse, lips twitching nervously as she forced a smile.

Bit of a change. The Sonja I'd originally met was a bitch. And even when she confessed to being blackmailed, she had more spine than this. I caught myself frowning and forced my forehead smooth as her smile faded.

"Hello, Syd," she said in a voice vibrating with anxiety, though she plastered on her fake happy again. "Can we talk?"

I had nothing to say to her, sneaking around behind my back, telling Liam who-knew-what. "Sure," I said, reaching for my door handle. "Come on in."

Contrary, yup. That was me all the way.

Charlotte rumbled unhappily as I entered my dorm room without looking back to see if Sonja was going to follow. Normally, my bodywere stayed out of my personal space, both at home and school. But I wasn't surprised to find the now brunette werewolf hovering at the door looking dangerous when I turned around to face Liam's mother.

Sonja threw a nervous glance at Charlotte who slowly,

oh so slowly, closed the door with one hand, eyes shifting to wolf and back again.

"Okay," I said, ignoring Sonja's discomfort, knowing it was incredibly uncharitable of me, but unable to shake my irritation at the whole sneaky mess she and Liam created around Venner. "You wanted to talk? So talk."

Sonja sank into my desk chair, her perfectly styled flippy cut showing off blonde highlights in her dark auburn hair. She was the epitome of a stylist with her flawless makeup and manicure, hair a piece of art. She'd used her job to shuffle Liam from town to town his whole life, keeping him away from Wilding Springs after his father died. And away from his grandfather and the knowledge Liam was the next Gatekeeper.

While I guessed I could understand her motivation, the fact she caved to Venner in the end and was part of the scheme reducing Fergus to debilitating dementia did little to ingratiate me to her. While I got it, her lack of backbone really pissed me off for some reason.

Probably because I'd put my own butt on the line for those I loved time and time again. Weakness in others seemed to be a touchstone for my temper.

"I wanted to come in person," Sonja said while my mind spun around my annoyance and the realization I had serious judgment issues. "To apologize."

"For?" Man, way to be a real bitch, Syd.

Sonja looked down, eyes locked on her hands, white

knuckled around the strap of her purse. What was she so afraid of? As long as she didn't put Liam in danger again...

Right. Venner. I was an idiot.

"Liam was worried you'd be upset if you knew we were in touch again." Sonja shifted, her high heels scraping over the wooden floor. "We didn't exactly part under the best of terms."

"And if you're still working for Venner," I said, tone so cold I swore I saw white mist escape my lips, "the terms haven't changed."

Her shoulders twitched. "He's different, now," she said as if she really believed it.

Funny. I didn't.

"I wanted to tell you about Lord Venemeth myself," Sonja said. I liked her better when she treated me like crap. At least her spine showed.

Oh, Syd.

"Let me guess." I crossed my arms over my chest. "He told you not to."

"Not His Lordship," Sonja said. "Liam. You were dealing with so much at the time... he worries about you constantly."

Grunt. It was really hard to stay angry with her when so much sadness crossed her face. And while empathy wasn't always my strongest suit with those who stabbed me in the back, I felt myself coming down from my high horse and actually feeling sorry for her.

"It's okay," I said. "Liam and I are just friends. And you're his mother. He didn't owe me an explanation." Although, hiding Venner was another thing all together.

She smiled at me, lips twitching in anxiety, but the horrible, heavy sorrow had left her face, at least. "I knew you'd understand," she said. "No matter what I've done, it was all for Liam."

Uh-huh. I sank to my bed to put her at ease. "So mind telling me what happened after the whole Gate debacle? I was worried Venner would hurt you for betraying him."

Sonja shook her head, but not to deny me my answers. "He was angry, yes," she said. "But failure took so much out of him, Syd. He softened, accepted who he was and his fate, finally." Tears welled in her eyes, her smile more genuine and less forced. "I'm Unseelie," she said. "And with Lord Venemeth's help, I've learned to embrace my heritage."

I wished I could believe her. Could set aside my usual suspicions and walk away from the whole worry thing. But I just couldn't bring myself to take what she told me at face value. My own hackles were still up. And it didn't help Shaylee spluttered and muttered and shrieked her disgust in my head while Sonja spoke.

Considering how many times I'd been right? Yeah, I'd take suspicious, thanks.

Shaylee didn't often talk to me, not because she

couldn't. So when she did, I sat up and paid attention.

Glamour, she snarled. One word. But enough.

I was an idiot.

Before I could reach out and touch Sonja with my power, something I should have thought to do if I hadn't been so damned busy being a self-righteous Miss Judgy Pants, someone knocked heavily on the door. Charlotte let out a yip of unhappiness, spinning to jerk it open.

Hortense Spaft brushed past my bodyguere as if Charlotte wasn't there, entering my room like she owned the place. A small smile devoid of anything humorous— or human, for that matter—pulled at the corners of her thin lips. Her endless black eyes glaring at me through her shining glasses, hair pulled back into her trademark bun, so tight her skin shone from the tension.

A shudder of absolute revulsion passed over me, but I forced myself to rise slowly as she came to a halt, trademark black wool suit and cream blouse making her look like the librarian at a haunted mansion.

"Miss Hayle." How I despised her voice. Those two simple words grabbed me by the throat and threw me back two years, to high school. Detention. Being forced to apologize over and over in a letter to her, polishing it to her liking before being allowed to leave. Hate I'd only felt in her presence rose in my heart and blacked out everything.

"Ms. Spaft." My shields vibrated around me, power

bubbling in my core, just waiting for an excuse.

Any excuse.

Instead of prodding me, she approached Sonja, firmly pulling the woman to her feet with a tight grip of her thin, white hand. I imagined a bloated, albino spider locking itself around Sonja's flesh and couldn't control the lip curl of disgust.

If Ms. Spaft noticed or cared, she didn't say anything. "Sonja, dear," she said in her grating voice that would make even the gentlest person look for the means to defend themselves. "We really must be going."

Sonja bobbed her head, tears forgotten. "Of course," she said.

Puppet, Shaylee hissed.

But whose? "It was nice to see you, Sonja," I said. Loudly. Like a challenge.

She blinked and smiled at me. "You too, Syd," she said.

Totally thralled. But as much as I wanted to, I knew what Mom would say if I tried to interfere. This wasn't any of my business. And yet it was.

Wasn't it?

Even if it wasn't, when had I ever let something like a little jurisdiction issue stop me before?

Ms. Spaft didn't wait, comment, nothing. Maybe she knew I was on to the fact Sonja wasn't all there or maybe she was just following orders. But even as I started to formulate a plan to somehow free Sonja from the evil woman, Ms. Spaft steered Liam's mother out the door and they were gone.

CҺAPTER SIX

I took my suspicions to Mom, sharing them with her over a freshly baked chocolate cake I brought with me from a cute little bakery on Harvard Square. I could tell from the guarded look in her eyes and the tightness of her smile she was onto me and the gooey offering I set on the table in her small kitchen, but that didn't stop her from fetching a pair of forks from the silverware drawer after Charlotte shook her head at the offer of a third. I set out a single glass, filled it with milk for us to share, the carton left out as I knelt on my chair and helped myself to a big bite, not even bothering to cut it first.

Mom sighed and dug in herself, a shadow passing over her face. My eyes drifted to her empty neck and I found myself frowning too. She'd lost her pentagram necklace last year and, despite the fact Meira and I replaced it, Mom never wore the new one. Made me a little angry, actually. Like our present didn't matter to her or wasn't good enough. I knew such thinking was just my reaction to her lack of enthusiasm for my visit, but bitterness was an old buddy I still hung out with from time to time, despite everything I'd learned about myself.

How could I kick it to the curb when we had so much history?

"I know what you're going to say." Mom jabbed at me, chocolate icing clinging to the tines of her fork. "I thought we agreed to observe until we knew more."

"There is more," I said, tapping the polished silver of my own fork against the tabletop in irritation before hooking off another large bite from the chocolate layers. "It's about Liam's mother," I said through a mouthful.

"Don't talk with food in your mouth," Mom said, attacking the cake and stuffing in her own large bite. "What about her?" A few crumbs flew as she ignored her own order.

"Shaylee thinks she's been glamoured." I swallowed, taking a long drink of milk.

Mom's eyebrows shot up as she chewed, but she remained silent until after she took her own drink, the glass thudding back to the table.

"You have proof?"

Proof shmoof. Mom knew me better than that. Proof and I had a very testy relationship. But I was always right, damn it. Wasn't I?

Shaylee grumbled in my head while I sat back, stomach churning too much to enjoy the sweet cake any longer. "Not yet," I growled. "But I'll get it."

"Syd." Mom leaned forward, pushing the cake aside, dropping her fork to take my hand. "Even if she is." She drew a deep breath before letting it out very slowly. "Even if she's under glamour, as long as it's Sidhe glamour, there's nothing we can do about it."

She did *not* just tell me such a thing.

"Mom," I used her exact same tone, setting sparks off in her eyes. Button successfully pushed. It had been a long time since we'd had a nuclear meltdown. And while I didn't really want to shove my mother into a corner, damn it, she needed to learn to listen to me. "This is Liam's *mother.*" I grit my teeth, sugary yumminess turning sour in my mouth. "Liam. The Gatekeeper." Pause for effect. "Mom."

She sat back, looking away, face creased in a scowl though I could tell from the way her lips twitched she struggled with what I said. Of course she understood.

"Lord Venemeth," she ground his name out without meeting my eyes, "has made powerful friends, Syd."

"Maybe he glamoured them, too." I wouldn't put it past him, the slippery slime ball.

"I can assure you," Mom's head swiveled around, angry blue eyes meeting mine, "I considered that possibility and, unlike you, it seems, I investigated before accusing."

Oh. My. Swearword.

I had buttons too. Still active after all this time.

"Not one of his supporters shows any sign of tampering," Mom said. "None." She looked like the fact hurt her, which made me feel a little better. "So there is nothing. I. Can. Do."

"What's the good of being Council Leader if you can't act?" My frustration with her churned in my stomach along with the cake, body wanting to reject both. "How many times will you stand by and let something terrible happen, Mom? When you could have acted before I had to clean up the mess?"

Mom's chair made a horrible scraping sound as she lurched to her feet, towering over me with her power rippling around her.

"I can't!" I'd never heard her so furious, so desperate. So full of despair. "Don't you understand? I can't." Mom's hands shook as her tone quieted, both pressed to her chest as she sank into her seat again. I caught Charlotte backing off out of the corner of my eye and wondered just how bad it looked and felt if my bodywere was about to come to my rescue against my own mother.

"Mom." I forced myself to calm the hell down and pull up my big girl panties. "I'm sorry." And I was, honest. I didn't think I could do her job, bound by rules and laws and stupid politics. I'd last about two seconds before they'd either burn me at the stake or the whole shebang would become a dictatorship under Queen Syd the Only.

Hell yeah.

Mom nodded while I pulled myself together. "I'm doing what I can inside the law," she said. Her blue eyes met mine, now full of sorrow. "Don't you think I wish I could just act without concern? I know he's a threat, Syd. But trying to convince those he's wooed is like beating my head against a brick wall."

Sympathy choked me a moment, joined by frustration and a healthy dose of guilt.

"I have Enforcers watching him," Mom said. "And there is no Gate here at Harvard for him to access. And as long as we keep an eye on him," she reached for my hand again, squeezed it, "there's nothing else either of us can do."

I almost pulled away. "You mean, that *you* can do."

Mom released my hand. "I've protected you in the past," she said. "Even though I knew you were right, Syd, you've gone against the law. You've included other races in witch matters and become embroiled in them yourself. Do you have any idea how much work it's taken me to smooth over the whole Europe incident?" Oh, like it was my fault the vampire Queens decided to kidnap me. Yeah, whatever. "Or the fact you were accused of murdering your demon grandmother?" How the hell did

47

they find out about Ahbi, anyway? "Not to mention the countless small infractions I hear about every single day." She rubbed her forehead with both hands. "Please don't misunderstand." When she dropped her arms, she was smiling, a soft, sad little smile. "You've done more to protect this plane, and others, than anyone else. But I'm forced to follow the mandate of my office."

"You accepted the job," I said, sympathy fading. "It was your choice, Mom."

Anger flashed on her face again. "I'm not complaining," she bit back. "I'm explaining." Her jaw worked, lips vibrating. "And were another witch the head of this Council, you would have been brought before a conclave long before now."

Whoa. "Just let them try."

"I don't want to give them a chance, Syd!" She was on her feet again, pacing, hugging herself. I glanced at Charlotte, seeing the concern flicker over the weregirl's face as she met my eyes. "Just for once, play by the rules. Please." Mom stopped and stared at me, hands falling to her sides. "Think of the family, your coven. Don't give anyone more reason to question your ability to lead."

My heart paused, fluttered. Beat again as my entire body went cold. Now that my anger had chilled out, I finally absorbed what she was saying. "Mom," I said. "What the hell?"

She slowly sat, hands in her lap, face falling into

weariness. "You scare them, sweetheart," she said. Barked a sudden laugh that made me jump. "You scare me sometimes, you know that?" I shook my head as she went on. "And if they fear you, they will try to destroy you. You have to believe that."

"This is ridiculous." Talk about ungrateful. Maybe it was time to stop saving the Council's sorry asses, all of witchdom. Let them catch fire and burn in their own filth.

Okay then. But not okay. Not by a long shot off a short pier.

"Fine," I said, shoulders slumping even as I felt my soul shrivel at the thought of giving up, of caving. "But when the bad crap happens and the whole show falls apart, do you think any of them will step up to do what needs to be done?"

She shook her head. "I know they won't," she whispered.

Just. Freaking. Lovely.

chapter seven

I didn't sleep very well that night. Tossing and turning courtesy of Shaylee. My demon. My vampire.

My own anger.

Shenka was already asleep when I arrived back at our dorm room, and it was just as well. I didn't have time to deal with her weird coldness from earlier at lunch, not with my head spinning and my temper rising now that I was out of Mom's reach.

They are fools, my vampire sent with heat, showing her rare temper.

Agreed, my demon snarled.

Venemeth is evil, Shaylee spat.

Tell me something I didn't know. *If Mom's worried*, I sent to them, *there's good reason. Why hadn't she told me how much trouble I'd been causing her?*

Probably because it wouldn't have changed anything, my

vampire sent. *You've done only what comes as natural—saved them all from destruction over and over again. Imagine if we hadn't been there to prevent Batsheva from the inevitable destruction of Pannera and her blood clan?*

Or the discovery of the Brotherhood infiltration in the European Council, Shaylee sent.

Or the Brotherhood's pursuit of domination. My demon chuffed softly. *Like any of the Council or other leaders are prepared to step up when the time comes.*

And yet. My vampire's anger cooled. *I agree with your mother on one thing, Sydlynn. Because I've felt similar animosity and almost let it destroy me.*

They are afraid of me. I rolled over on my side, hugging my pillow.

Fear is a powerful enemy, my vampire sent. *History is full of examples of society destroying their saviors out of misplaced fear.*

So what are we supposed to do, then? My demon growled, twisting inside me while Shaylee hunched deep, earth magic thrumming, making me feel ten times as heavy. *Nothing?*

Of course not, my vampire sent. *But we must be more cautious. And have answers prepared in case we are asked to defend ourselves.*

I don't know if you've noticed, I sent, feeling a hysterical giggle building inside me, *but we don't exactly do caution and advanced planning very well.*

For once, she didn't chastise me for my humor. *Indeed,*

she sent with a hint of her own laughter. *But perhaps it's something we need to learn.*

Sigh.

I finally slept while my alter egos grumbled and settled. One thing was for sure—Mom's warning was just that. And she was right about putting the coven first. I felt a sharp jab of protectiveness for my family, knowing how much I risked them and their futures.

And yet, I didn't have a choice.

No self-pity. I was way past those days of falling into a black pit of boo-hoo. But a healthy dose of "why me" would have been nice, just this once.

Shenka was gone when I finally woke, groggy and out of sorts, the sun streaming in cheerful beams across my face.

Not feeling even remotely perky, I forced myself into the shower for a quick scrub before slumping my way down to the Yard and heading for breakfast. Charlotte remained silent through our walk, her usual. And though there were times I wished she'd talk to me, carry on a normal conversation, this wasn't one of those times. Her quiet suited me perfectly.

My friends were already assembled, chatting over breakfast, when I approached with my tray. It took me a full three breaths of absolute shock to comprehend my normal place next to Liam was full.

Of Tippy.

What?

The only place left was at the end of the table, between Josie and Nicci. And while I liked them both, it wasn't the same. Shenka sat on Liam's left, in Tippy's usual seat.

And the red haired wench with the big boobs she better stop brushing against his arm sat where I was supposed to be.

Worse? Liam, who normally blushed and turned away from her flirting, leaned close to the tart and laughed, whispering in her ear while she giggled and squeezed his bicep with her manicured hands.

Appetite successfully slain.

"Oh, hey, Syd!" Tippy waved with her plastic spoon, smiling like she wasn't the worst kind of vile traitor, her red hair falling across Liam's hand, her shoulder pressed to his. And didn't I just know her hot little thigh was cemented to his faded jeans?

I sank into the empty seat and stared at her. "Hi." One word. All I could manage. Liam glanced up, met my eyes, looked away.

Without even a hint of guilt. Or recognition. Or friendliness.

I wondered how he'd look with my yogurt all over his stupid white t-shirt.

Conversation went on without me, as though I weren't even there, like my social world had done an abrupt about face and slammed me into a cement wall. There was a time I was forced into the life of a loner, when I wanted friends more than anything, something normal to cling to. And then a time I chose to be alone, where having friends to care about was too complicated. But I'd become complacent, accepted I could have people around me who treated me like I was just another witch.

The loner thing was looking pretty good again.

"Syd," Tippy gushed at me, leaning over so far I could see the crumb of toast in her cleavage. Way down in her cleavage. Seriously. "We need to chat about my audition. I can't wait to show you what I can do for you and your coven."

Like she had even the remotest chance now that she'd wrapped her disgusting little paws around my...

Choke.

My what? My Liam? But he wasn't my Liam, was he? He was right what he said yesterday. I'd told him time and again we couldn't be together. And yet, here I was going all jealous crazy.

What did that say about me and how I felt about him?

Sigh.

More to ponder. Punctuated by frustration when Shenka stood up without looking at me and stomped off. Damn her. Like I needed more drama.

Still, what was his problem? The Liam I knew wouldn't turn tables so fast. I pondered the possibility

Tippy was influencing him, refusing to believe he would purposely torture me over our earlier conversation about his mother.

He just wouldn't.

It took a supreme effort to jerk myself under control and force a smile on my face in answer to Tippy.

"We'll see," I said, my eyes going to Liam's face again even as he turned to push his breakfast around with his fork. Looked like I wasn't the only one without much of an appetite. He finally set down his utensil and sat back, passing one big hand over his face as his cheeks paled a little.

"Are you okay?" Panic rippled around me despite my irritation with his about-face as Shaylee instantly reached for him, but he blocked us with his own magic and frowned, finally meeting my eyes.

"I'm fine," he said, climbing to his feet, slinging his backpack over his shoulder. "Coming, Tips?"

She wriggled herself out of her chair and linked arms with him, giant bag in her free hand. "You betcha, handsome." Her broad wink at me as they walked away lit the fire of my fury all over again.

When I looked back, I found Donalda watching me. "If you call poaching," she said, "we'll all back you."

So the other girls noticed, did they? What I'd taken for coldness toward me was just the opposite. I reached out and grabbed Donalda's hand, squeezed it before releasing her and taking Nicci's and finally Josie's.

"He's fair game," I said, hating to say it, but knowing it was true. I finally embraced what I'd been asking Liam to accept all along. "No foul."

All three girls stared a moment before Donalda shrugged and tsked softly.

"If you can't see how much he loves you," she said, gathering her own things while the other two joined her, "I guess Tippy deserves him after all."

I sat in stunned silence, feeling tears burn my eyes, the scent of breakfast making my stomach heave even as the warmth of the sun through the stained glass windows did nothing to dispel the shiver of goosebumps I rubbed away with rough hands.

Charlotte's low growl was the only warning I had, no time to pull myself out of sadness and into guarded anger in time. Venner sat next to me while Charlotte hummed her unhappiness, but I waved her off, hating he'd seen me vulnerable.

He didn't comment, at least. Would have lost something important to his survival if he had. Instead, he smiled his little smirk at me, green eyes sparkling as he toyed with the long, silver length of his hair, a large ring flashing on his right hand.

"I must say I was delighted to see you yesterday." Yeah, right. Though, maybe he was. Shaylee spit and shrieked in my head, making it hard to focus. "The absolute delight on your face warmed my heart, Your Highness."

Bastard. "I hope it keeps you warm at night," I said, teeth flashing as I bared them in a viscous grin. "Considering you don't have many nights left to enjoy yourself."

Venner reached out and patted my hand, putting his life in imminent danger. Not just from me, but from Charlotte. I could feel the wolf in her struggling to emerge, to tear his throat out with her teeth. And while the vision was inspiring, my demon and Shaylee adding to the gory details, I had Mom's warning to think about.

"I find your little Council so quaint," he said, tapping his long, thin fingers on the tabletop. "And the board of governors." He snorted elegantly—I'd never heard anyone manage it, but he did, the ass—and cupped his cheek in his free hand. "They adore me. So much. How lovely."

"Lovely," I echoed between clenched teeth. "I hate games, Venner. Just put your damned cards on the table and stop jerking my chain."

"Oh, but doing so delights me." He reached out for me again, took one of my hands in both of his, the cool, smooth skin creeping me out hard core. His lips brushed my knuckles as his large green eyes sparked with Sidhe magic. "And I'd hate to ruin the surprise too soon."

"If you touch Liam," I snarled, pushing forward until

our noses practically touched, "or go one step near the Gate or anyone I care about, I will personally dismember you and hide your body parts where no one will ever find them."

Venner's eyes shuttered over, darkening, though his smirk remained. "Such class," he said. "Wherever did you get your manners, Miss Hayle?"

I'd show him manners. But before I could say or do anything further, Venner rose in a single graceful movement, a slip of paper falling on my tray.

"I'll see you at my lecture tomorrow morning," he said as he drifted off. "Tardiness will not be accepted."

I watched him go even as Charlotte lunged over my shoulder and retrieved the note. She didn't unfold it, just lifted it to her nose and sniffed. Her eyes flickered to wolf and back again before she growled in disgust.

"What?"

She handed me the paper, her wolf retreating. "No scent," she said.

"Isn't that kind of impossible?" Not to doubt her nose, but Charlotte's was the keenest I'd ever come across.

Except. Except when it came to one person in particular. Ever since Harvard last year and the vampire incident, Charlotte's sensitivity for my most hated enemy was left in the dark.

Charlotte held the note out to me and I accepted it

from her, anxiety mixing with rising anger.

Two unfolds later and I had my confirmation no scent could mean only one thing.

I told you I knew about Liam.

See you on the Green.

A.

chapter eight

I ran all the way to Coven Hall, Charlotte right behind me, wanting to ride the veil, but hearing Mom's voice in my head, begging me to play it cool even as the terror I felt at Ameline's cryptic note drove spikes of panic through my chest.

The last time she'd contacted me about someone I cared about, I'd found my demon grandmother dead in her apartments and was accused of her murder. So I didn't think anyone would blame me for the blinding fear gripping me as I raced after Liam.

Only to crash into his back as he stopped to allow Tippy through the door ahead of him. Liam turned, frowning a little, hazel eyes flat as his strawberry blonde hair hung over his forehead. But his gaze lightened as though he only then realized I was there. He reached for me as I staggered, concern rising in his face in answer to what had to have been open terror on mine.

"Syd." He hugged me gently before letting me go, the old Liam back again. Now that I knew Ameline was involved, I immediately suspected she had something to do with his actions this morning. "What's wrong?"

I touched his cheek with trembling fingers, feeling how cold and clammy he was, internally snorting at my last thought. Like she'd be so petty to try to turn Liam against me. I knew she had to have bigger fish to reel in. But his physical condition amped up my worry. "Are you feeling okay?"

He snuffled a little, nodding. "Just getting a cold," he said. "I'm fine."

A cold. Right. But when I tried to probe him with magic, he gently but firmly blocked me again.

"I'm fine, Syd," he said. Smiled a little, the smile I—sigh—loved. "You worry too much, you know that?"

My fear level dropped a bit as he slung one arm around my shoulders, the familiar scent of earth and his laundry calming me.

Right.

We walked over the entry together, through the magic doorway to Coven Hall's main corridor. I waved at him as he left me, missing the warmth of his arm over my shoulder, wondering where his coldness from breakfast had gone, but happy it seemed to have passed. I watched as he moved through a door on his way to class, leaving me to stand there and fret over him before just making it through the closing portal to my own class before it sealed shut.

As hard as I tried to track Liam down all day, he evaded me, and I wondered if Tippy had something to do with it after all. She was nice enough in lab, chattering on about how amazing she'd be as my second, but the moment we were set free, she latched onto my Sidhe—friend?—and took off. And though I was sure she wouldn't be so stupid to use magic on Liam, why else had he made such a sudden about face?

Because I'd been a jerk about his mom. Time to face the fact I could only reject him so many times, prod him and try to—gulp—control him in the name of keeping him safe before he'd had enough. Liam was sweet, kind and gentle. But even he had to have his limit.

Maybe I'd just hit it.

Misery, thy name is Syd.

After one last failed attempt to talk to him, finding his dorm room empty that night and not wanting to think about the fact he was probably with—didn't want to think about it—her, I found a seat on a bench at the edge of the Yard and tried to quell the returning fear squeezing my chest so tight I could barely breathe.

Power whooshed, air parting only feet from me, discharging a handful of black-robed Enforcers into the Yard. One of them turned, chocolate eyes meeting mine

62

and, before I knew it, Quaid waved to the departing group and made his way toward me.

Just what I needed. A Quaid lecture.

My day would be complete.

At least he didn't dive into accusing me of looking for trouble right away. Nope. He lulled me into a false sense of security by frowning as he sat and taking my hand.

"You look like you need a shoulder," he said.

Normally, this would cue tears and hopeless sobbing. At least, from the old me.

Okay, maybe for the new me, too. I felt my eyes prickle with tears, my throat tighten, but I held off, rigid and tense. To his credit, Quaid didn't pull away, sitting back with my hand still in his strong, warm one, letting his power out ever so gently to wrap around mine. My demon welcomed him, pulled him close as I fell back into the familiar circle of his arms.

"Rough day?" Quaid's deep, rumbling voice vibrated between us.

I'd missed his voice. His magic. The power of his embrace. The way his body felt when we—

Oh, Syd.

I shook off the sadness rising at what could have been and answered him. "You could say that," I said. "You too?"

He shrugged, resting his cheek on my hair. "Yes," he said. "And no."

It had been so long since I'd just sat in a comfortable silence, I actually felt a little angry when he spoke again.

"So what's up?" His thumb gently rubbed the back of my hand, arm tightening around my shoulder.

Yeah, like I was falling for the trap that would lead to his inevitable judging. "Nothing I can't handle," I said, more sharply than I intended. But he hadn't had my back in the past, not the recent past, anyway. And I wasn't in the mood to hear him pontificate about how much of a screw up he thought I was.

Instead of the jab about being a trouble magnet I expected, Quaid sighed. "I'm sorry, you know," he said into my hair. "About how many times I've doubted you."

This was new. "You should be." Nice, Syd.

Quaid's chuckle made my demon purr and stretch her power toward him. I shut her down. No way was I ending up in his bed just because she thought he was being nice.

For once.

"Just tell me," he said. "I swear I won't say a word."

Against my better judgment, knowing I was making a colossal mistake and would end up calling him all kinds of mean names in my head and likely out loud because of it, I dumped my worries on him. All of them. About Ameline, Venner, Liam, Sonja. Ms. Spaft. All of it. Quaid was good to his word, keeping his damned mouth shut until I wound down with Mom's warning.

And my own fear for the coven, whispered in the

dark.

"What if I ruin it for the family, Quaid?" I met his eyes at last, tears welling, but not embarrassed by them. "I've never had a choice, have I? But maybe I have." I sniffed, wiped at the moist track down my cheek. "Maybe you've been right all along and if I hadn't butted my nose in, none of this would have happened."

Quaid let out a gusty sigh and turned his body toward me, releasing his hold so he could grip my upper arms and shake me, ever so gently. "Syd," he said. "Stop being an idiot."

I tried to pull away, but he was too strong, enfolding me in his arms, pressing me against his broad chest, the scent of him all rich and lovely filling my world until I just let him hold me.

"You're the bravest person I've ever met," he said, shocking me right down to the tips of my toes. "And I promise you, no matter what happens, if you need me, for anything, you just ask. And I'll be there."

Big words. "Until you can't be," I said.

He was silent a moment before he spoke again, voice thick with emotion. "Of all the things I regret most in my life," he said, "saying no to you is the worst." I wasn't about to encourage him, but then again, this supportive Quaid disarmed me enough I stayed where I was and listened. "I've seen things, Syd," he went on, words dropping low and quiet in the darkness, "things I can't even describe." His chuckle warmed me, sent zinging sparks through my blood. "I've even made my own trouble a few times." Hot lips found my temple, the heat of his breath adding to the thrill of fire coursing all over me. "I will never let anything slide again." More sadness. He was running the gamut of emotions with me tonight.

"Thank you," I whispered. Cleared my throat. Tried again. "I'm really worried about Liam."

Quaid's whole body tensed and he half pushed me away before his head dropped, shoulders slumping under his black robe. Way to ruin the connection, Hayle. "I know," he said, yet another surprise from Mr. Sarcasm. "And from the sounds of things, you should be. Have you told your mother?"

"I don't have any proof, remember? Just a mysterious note. I know it's from her. But that 'A' could be interpreted otherwise." I missed Quaid's warmth as he turned away, gaze lost in the distance.

"Then we'll find some." He turned back, smiled, a real smile, not the smirk I always wanted to wipe from his handsome face.

I have no idea why I brought her up. Except maybe with Liam hanging between us, it reminded me. "How's Payten?" I said it softly, gently even, but my mention of his tawny-haired "friend" made him frown.

"I don't know," he said. "We're not together. And I've been away on assignment."

I wondered how long the situation would last, now that he was back.

My question finally shattered the last of our togetherness. Quaid stood, offered his hands and I accepted them, feeling a bit better at least, if guilty for wrecking a perfectly good moment. We had so few of those, he and I.

I felt him hesitate before he bent over me, lips brushing across mine. I could have had more. Could have gone with him back to his room, spent the night with him, allowed my demon to have her way. But I wasn't that kind of girl and the agreement we'd had, to just love each other, felt thin and cold there in the darkness.

"Keep me posted," he whispered over my lips before leaving me, disappearing into the Yard, while I hugged myself and wondered if I'd ever allow myself to get over him.

CHAPTER NINE

Shenka wasn't even in our room when I arrived home and didn't show up until long after I went to bed. I almost confronted her on her cone of silence, but just didn't have the energy.

Drama. Jeeze, did I hate drama.

Instead, I lay in bed and focused on the next morning and my alternating worry about something diabolical happening during Venner's lecture and the fear I was overreacting, after all, and putting Mom and Quaid on edge for no good reason.

All I had to do was think about the note Ameline sent and I swayed back to the diabolical.

What had she meant? That she knew about Liam? It was the second time she'd said it, once in person, now in a note. Knew what? I assumed she was aware he was the Gatekeeper. Kind of hard to keep that little tidbit a secret, honestly. And if she was in contact with Venner, even more so. What was it she knew I didn't—or wasn't taking seriously enough?

Fretting never suited me but I couldn't seem to avoid it.

The fact Ameline was working with Venner, or more likely, he was working for her, only made things worse. Even if Venner wasn't up to something, even if I'd horribly misjudged him, there was no way Ameline's involvement spelled anything but trouble.

And while I lay there and told myself I had to alert Mom about this new development, there was no proof.

No. Proof. A note signed with a single letter "A" only I could identify as Ameline. I could have put Charlotte's nose, the fact she didn't smell a thing, an impossibility only tied to Ameline, but she was a werewolf. Not a witch. And the lack of a scent wasn't much in the way of concrete evidence anyway.

How much did this politics stuff suck?

Another night with little sleep left me grumpy and out of sorts, but at least Shenka fled early yet again and saved me the effort to be nice to her despite her frigid treatment of me. I grumbled out loud around my toothbrush at my reflection in the mirror, but the conversation got me nowhere except in a fouler mood.

Peachy.

I avoided breakfast, not wanting to go through the

whole Tippy and Liam scene again, instead stopping at the on-campus cafe for a banana and a bran muffin, eating my cold and tasteless meal alone while my mind churned around the possibilities. If I wasn't going to be able to act, things could get very bad, very quickly. And though I knew I had to do something if the need arose, would I now hesitate, flinch, thinking about Mom and her warning?

Would it blunt my edge? Because in a lot of cases, my edge was all I had to keep me alive.

I really needed to find a new hobby besides giving myself an ulcer over things I couldn't control.

Coven Hall buzzed with excitement as I entered, only one door open and available for entry. The massive lecture theater on the other side looked familiar, in that it shared the same décor as every other classroom on witch campus, but was three times the size of what I was used to. The little trick Coven Hall used to only allow students into their assigned classes seemed to be able to alter the size and shape of the rooms themselves.

I spotted Liam and Tippy, Shenka huddled next to them, near the middle of the room. Nicci looked up and waved, but I just couldn't bring myself to sit with them. I waved back, wondering how I could avoid them without hurting more feelings when I spotted a familiar face three rows back, dark brown gaze fixed on me. I pointed at Quaid so Nicci would understand and saw her turn, spot him, then roll her eyes at me with a wink. Let her think what she wanted. All of my friends heard some version of my Quaid saga, so she was well aware I still waffled when it came to him.

Let Liam choke on it.

Syd. Bad, Syd. Bad.

I spotted Mom as I slid through the row toward Quaid. She sat at the front with the rest of the Council and the three board of governors members I'd met. I flopped into my seat just as Tippy pointed back over her shoulder. Liam turned around and spotted me. My first thought was how pale he seemed, cheeks hollowed out, bags under his eyes. My second was irritation at the flash of jealousy passing over his face.

He did *not* get to be jealous. No. Freaking. Way.

It didn't help matters Quaid grinned, waving at his rival. Seriously? Children, both of them. I jabbed handsome and jerkly in the ribs as Liam turned back around with a surly look on his face.

"If you don't mind," I snapped. "Can you focus, please?"

"Just having some fun." Quaid's smirk had made a comeback.

Fun. Holy. "Grow up," I said. "Or get lost."

He must have known I meant it. I was so tired of the pair of them battling over something neither of them could have, the way they were acting. Not without my permission, anyway.

"You're right," Quaid said, sitting back. "Sorry. He just makes me..."

"What?" I dumped my backpack on the floor, still zipped, not even thinking about taking notes. Shaylee knew more about the Sidhe than poser Venner could ever dream.

Her thought. Not mine.

My Seelie princess had an attitude. Surprise, surprise.

The place filled quickly, almost every seat taken, the full complement of students chattering in excitement as the door finally swung shut. I wondered, looking around me at the innocent faces, the rim of Enforcers lining the hall, if any of them had any idea just how dangerous their new teacher really was.

Or that he worked for someone worse.

I almost missed the grand entrance, and trust me, missing it would have taken some doing. Venner swept into the center of the lecture space in a rush of green fire, perfectly tailored charcoal suit a stunning counterpoint to his shining silver hair and milk-white complexion. Ms. Spaft appeared at his right hand to the gasps of most of the watching students. Did Mom's shoulders twitch at the pompous showmanship? Or did I imagine it?

I knew her better than that. Mine jerked in answer.

"Students," Venner began, his voice velvet and mist, power rumbling through the floor in a soft vibration of earth magic, "board of governors," he bowed to the three ladies and several more, all of whom waved to him, "and High Council," again with the sweeping bend at the waist. Mom didn't move. "I thank you for this invitation to guest lecture at the revered and honored Coven Hall."

Perfect mix of arrogance and humility. He had them eating out of his slim-fingered hands.

I have no idea what Ms. Spaft's role was. Not with Venner launching into a grandiose speech about his people and the goals of the lecture series. I really didn't pay attention to a word he said. Shaylee did, better believe it, and I had to snap at her on occasion over the next ninety minutes so I could focus. Hard to do while she snarled and snorted and called him names.

His power continued to embrace the whole hall, but that was it. At least as far as I could tell. It just sat there in a pool beneath us, humming.

Anything? Quaid's mental voice broke my concentration.

Nothing. Grumpy Syd was grumpy. There had to be something. Some proof. Some plan.

Just stay focused, Quaid sent, which triggered an internal tirade he really didn't want to hear.

Really, really.

It wasn't until the final moments of the lecture Shaylee stopped swearing and judging and started paying attention. And when she did, I felt what I'd missed without her. The power beneath us wasn't dormant. Not precisely. Ever so subtle, it radiated outward, a soft kiss of magic, touching each and every soul in the room.

My eyes widened as I looked around and caught traces of green Sidhe power. The barest hints here and there, but not everywhere. Just around certain students and faculty.

Do you see that? I jabbed Quaid's mind.

What? He looked around quickly. *What are you seeing?*

He's doing something with his magic, I sent back as my soul crowed. Finally, proof! But of what? The green tendrils didn't damage anyone they touched, just softly explored their surface. It wasn't until Shaylee's touch drifted over the closest of Venner's victims I understood what was going on.

I could see it because of Shaylee. Because, like me, like her, the dozen or so souls in the hall who Venner's power tracked had Sidhe blood, too. It was confirmed to me when a rope of magic slid up Liam's back and stroked his hair before falling away.

I had no idea why Venner needed to track Sidhe carriers at my school. But no way was it for good reasons.

He's locating those with Sidhe blood, I sent, stomach cramping with nerves.

Why? Quaid tensed beside me. *What good will that do him?*

I don't know, I sent, *but I'm about to show him it's a very bad idea.*

Shaylee didn't wait for me. She snaked her power down the rows to the source of the explorations and cut Venner's magic off like she turned off a faucet.

Everyone jumped when the hum of earth magic ended abruptly. Venner met my eyes, smiled at me even from the distance and bowed to my mother just as the ending chime sounded.

"And that," he said, "is our lesson for today."

Just what had *he* learned?

chapter ten

I stayed in my seat, Quaid next to me, fuming while Venner shook hands with the board of governors and the Council. I noted Mom was the only exception, as she carefully dodged his outstretched hand with a diplomatic smile, moving another witch forward to take her place in a smooth but obvious snub.

There were times Mom and I didn't get along, and times I wished I was more like her.

Guess which this was.

I was less surprised than I should have been to spot Sonja standing just inside the now-open door, small next to the hulking Enforcers in their black robes. Liam spotted her about the same time I did and left Tippy to hurry through the departing crowd to hug his mother. I left my row more slowly, doing my best to keep an eye on Venner, Spaft and Sonja all at once while Quaid stayed close behind me, his scent and the heat of his body where he brushed against me a sizzling distraction.

Hormones? Really? At a time like this.

Classy.

I paused at the edge of the seats while Quaid passed me. Stopped. Bent and kissed me with such deliberation I didn't really enjoy it, knowing he had motive.

Okay, I enjoyed it. But I still wasn't happy about it when he pulled away.

"I have a trainee meeting," he said, hovering over my lips, rumbling voice cutting through me despite the raised level of noise as the student body trundled off. "But I'll see you later?" His voice caught at the end. As if he wasn't sure he was welcome.

Well, Syd? Was he?

If my demon had her way, that would be a hell, yeah. But I had other things to consider. Like my immortality. And his uncanny knack for abandoning me. And yet, it was Quaid, and my heart, my traitor of a heart, refused to let him go.

"Okay," I said, squeezing his hand, my lips smiling even as I fought to stay calm and level and not freak out over the attention he offered.

Lost.

Quaid's answering grin warmed me before he kissed me ever so gently one more time and spun, marching off.

I barely had time to sigh out the breath we'd shared

when Liam appeared at my side, towering over me, a scowling, strawberry blonde cloud of doom.

"What did he want?" Liam jerked one thumb in Quaid's departing direction. Like Liam hadn't just spent the last day or so flirting with Tippy. And hadn't given me the brush-off.

Sizzling desire for Quaid turned to snapping temper in a flash. "Nothing," I snapped. Lied. Knowing Quaid wanted a whole lot of something I wasn't sure I was willing to give anymore.

Liam's jealousy raised bright pink points on his cheeks, showing like blows on his pale face. His freckles stood out so much they almost seemed to float over his transparent flesh. He opened his mouth to argue with me only to catch himself with a coughing fit. My temper cooled immediately, worry for him pushing me forward to pat his back while he grasped my shoulder for balance, his other fist over his mouth.

Sonja appeared, looking as worried as I was, taking his free arm when he dropped his hand.

"We need to get you to bed," she said, Mom authority undeniable. There was no sign of the nervousness she showed me yesterday, all smooth and under control again. "You've caught a terrible bug, sweetie."

I reached for him with my magic, to offer healing, but this time it was Sonja's power holding me off. Her eyes met mine, a frown bending her mouth.

"I can take care of him," she said, as if I'd insulted her. Sonja then smiled kindly up at her tall son as he sighed and rubbed his forehead with one hand. "Come on, baby," she said. "Some of Mom's soup and some sleep will fix you up."

Soup? Was she kidding? The boy needed healing magic. Then again, it was just the flu. Stupid flu.

"Thank you for your concern, Syd," Sonja said over her shoulder, "but taking care of Liam is my responsibility now."

I watched the pair of them go, knowing I could probably help, but not sure I wanted to ease his suffering after all.

Petty, Syd. So petty.

Promising myself I'd check in later to sneak him some healing after all, I instead turned to catch Mom's eye. She looked up as my magic touched her and nodded just a bit.

We need to talk, I sent even as I dreaded it. *Venner is up to something.*

Her brows pulled together.

Syd, she sent, an edge of anger in her mental voice, *I watched him the entire time. And I felt nothing.* Her blue eyes narrowed. *Nothing.*

I know, I shot back, temper returning. *You're not Sidhe.*

What does that have to do with anything? Mom's exasperation actually pissed me off. I was doing my due diligence, wasn't I? And keeping my nose clean, passing off the information instead of tearing the slimy slime lord apart with my bare hands.

It means, Gram's voice cut in so suddenly I almost cried out, one hand pressed to my chest as Charlotte released a yip of surprise at my reaction, *you're being a fool again, Miriam. And it doesn't look good on you.*

Mom flinched, only enough I caught it. *Stay out of this, Mother.*

My grandmother, still back in Wilding Springs but tied to me for so many reasons I could hardly count, cackled in my head. *Things are quiet here*, she sent. *No big explosions or apocalypses to keep me company. I have to outsource for my entertainment.* Her mind hugged me. *Now*, the whip came out again, *listen to your daughter or I'll come to Harvard and kick your ass myself.*

Very well. I could tell Mom's irritation level was reaching critical, but with Gram on my side, at least I had backup. *What do you mean, Syd?*

He was looking for those with Sidhe ties. I waited for the gasp of surprise, didn't hear it from either of them. Okay then. *Quaid couldn't see it either, Mom. Because he isn't Sidhe. And if your Enforcers aren't descendants, they wouldn't see it either.*

Nor would anyone not looking for trouble, my vampire added her thoughts to the mix. *It was only because we were all watching we sensed it at all. I doubt very much the ones Venner examined have any idea they even have Sidhe blood.*

Mom fell quiet a moment before answering as she

faked a smile and nodded to one of the board of governors who spoke to her. *So*, she sent, *you're telling me you could see it, but no one else could?*

I could do without the heavy sarcasm, thanks.

Listen up, Ethpeal sent. *If he's searching out witches who carry Sidhe, he's definitely planning something. And Syd is correct in assuming only those with the heritage would be able to sense something like that.* I was pretty sure Gram was smudging the truth just to have my back, but I loved her for it. *So unless you have an Enforcer you can call on who has Sidhe blood, you're going to have to rely on Syd to watch this critter.*

Mom paused again, but when she spoke up this time, her anger was gone, replaced with weariness. *You're right, of course.* She sighed in my head, a heavy sound making me worry about her. *But with no evidence of wrongdoing outside Syd's word, there's nothing I can do. And Syd needs to keep her nose clean, Mother. You know that.*

They'd been talking about me behind my back, had they?

I know. Even Gram sounded subdued. *But there's no way any of us will stand by and watch this Unseelie lordling act if we can stop him.*

Agreed. Mom's magic hugged me, sliding around Gram's until the three of us were locked together. *I'll find out if any of my people have Sidhe blood*, Mom sent.

There's more. There was always more. *He's working with Ameline.*

Mom grunted her surprise. *You're sure?*

Did she just ask me that question for real?

Sorry, she sent. *Reflex. This changes things. But I take it you don't have proof or I would have heard by now.*

I hated it when she was right.

I told her about the note anyway, Charlotte's nose troubles. Won me a sigh and a mental headshake.

If *Ameline is involved.* Mom sounded like she didn't believe me. Imagine. *And I say if, Syd, she's not your responsibility. And until I can find someone to corroborate your findings, you'll just have to watch Venner. But be careful. And do not, under any circumstances, take action without telling me first. All right?*

I grumbled my agreement as Gram whispered support in my ear. *If you get a chance, take that bastard down.*

CHAPTER ELEVEN

I walked out of the lecture theater, mind churning, and into an argument.

Shenka practically chest bumped me as I exited the room, head down, and I had to jerk to a halt, squeaking in surprise for the second time. I was one of the last to leave, so at least I wasn't blocking the exit. Because the look on Shenka's face told me she wasn't letting me go until she spoke her mind.

Good then. A nice fight was just what I needed to work out the kinks.

"No hitting," I said.

Shenka's furious face fell as she blinked. "Sorry?"

"The fight we're about to have." I poked my thumb over my shoulder at Charlotte who eased past me, eyes locked on Shenka. "No hitting. Unless you want to end up pinned to the ground with a werewolf taking a chunk out of you."

Shenka shook her head, anger returning though more sullen and less apparent.

"I don't want to hit you," she said. Paused. "Okay, that's a lie."

I laughed a little, knowing it wasn't funny, but unable to stop myself. Shenka stomped one foot, her own anger leaving her.

"You're ruining it," she wailed.

"I'm sorry." I straightened my shoulders and nodded to Charlotte. "Try to hold back if she hits me, okay?"

Shenka giggled, eyes welling with tears before she sighed and slumped. "I'm sorry," she said. "I've just been so worked up about this."

"About what?" I took her arm and led her aside, out of the path of milling students now prepping to go to their classes. Doors appeared out of nowhere, the influx of teen witches and their teachers flowing around us.

Shenka wiped one wet cheek with the back of her hand. "Why did you ask Tippy to be your second?"

Um-hum. No shocker here. And yet... "I didn't," I said, rolling my eyes. "She found out I was looking and went all fangirl on me."

Shenka giggled again, her sadness lifting a bit, though I could tell there was much more to this. So I prodded her.

"You were the one who wouldn't talk about it," I

said. "I thought you didn't want the job anymore." And did I want her to have it? This was the second time she'd pulled away from me, that I'd had to wrangle her. Would she make a good second anyway?

Shenka drew a breath, shoulders straightening at last. "I must seem like a total wash to you now," she said, as if reading my thoughts. "But I swear, Syd, I'll make a great second. And I really, really want the job." Enthusiasm rose in her voice, a smile returning. Only to fade. "I just don't know how to tell Tallah." More tears. "I know being your second is the right thing for me. I've never felt so sure of anything in my life." She dashed at the tears with anger. "But how do I leave my sister?"

I hugged her quickly with my arms while doing the same with my magic. That embrace lasted long after I pulled away and nodded.

"I totally understand," I said. "We've talked about this, but not enough, obviously. Shenka, I know you'll do a great job," and it was true, my doubts melting away, "but if doing so means breaking up your family or hurting Tallah, I don't know if I can let you go through with it."

Shenka leaned against the wall, her book bag falling from one shoulder to land on the floor with a thump. "Tallah will get over it," she said. "It's telling her at all that's holding me back."

"Did you want me to talk to her with you?" A united front might make it easier for Shenka, but how would

Tallah react? I knew her as a friend, but I hadn't really seen her in action as a coven leader, other than during Mom's trial. The laid-back, kind-hearted Tallah I knew could easily freak out if the two of us confronted her.

I was willing to try, though.

But Shenka's sudden determination, her face now set in a small smile, brown eyes sparkling with resolve, told me she'd made her own decision.

"Thank you," she said. "But that's my job, isn't it? And I won't be much of a second to you if I can't stand up to my own sister."

"Will she bully you?" I didn't get that vibe from the sisters, but being pushed around came in many forms, sometimes too subtle for an outsider to see.

"In her way," Shenka said. "But I'm not a little girl anymore. And Mama would have wanted us both to be happy, no matter what Tallah thinks." Shenka grabbed her bag, slung it back over her shoulder while her smile softened. "I'll tell you about our mother sometime. And the stupid promise she made us make. Sometimes the best thing for a family is to go our separate ways."

I almost spoke up, almost told her no, that family came first. But selfishness won.

I watched Shenka march off, not to class, but out into Widener Library, knowing she went to talk to Tallah. Guilt warred with pride as I passed through the door to my next period, knowing I'd made a great choice after all.

chapter twelve

I waited at the exit to the library for Quaid for about ten minutes after classes ended for the day. When he didn't show, I kicked myself for even bothering. No more waiting around for stray boys to get their crap together, not when I had things to do.

Entirely unfair. Quaid's "see you later" hadn't had a time attached to it, outside "later."

Still.

Sniff.

I made a quick bag dump in my dorm, leaving my backpack behind. It didn't look like Shenka had been around, and I worried something happened between her and Tallah. She missed lunch, too, and I had to tolerate Tippy's gushing all over me with no Liam to hit on while the other girls eye-rolled and stayed quiet.

Charlotte didn't comment when I turned right back

around and left my room, heading out into the Yard. She must have known very well where I was off to, because she didn't miss a step when I turned abruptly and headed for Liam's dorm. It was a quick walk, but it felt like it took forever, now that I was heading his way.

A knock on his door didn't rouse a response, so I snooped. My magic curled under the lip, over the hardwood floor, a subtle thread I hoped Liam wouldn't take personally. Not that he usually would. My Sidhe friend was nothing if not kind and sweet at all times. Except lately. So what changed? Yes, he was sick. But before that...

Sonja. I couldn't bring myself to believe his own mother could turn him around so easily. Not when she had years to do so without anyone interfering.

Venner? If he was tampering with my friend, Mom or no Mom, threat to me or not, I'd be sending him back to the Unseelie Court, all right.

In a body bag.

Temper, Syd. Temper.

That left Ameline.

If she touched him, it would take her years to die from the pain I inflicted.

"Liam?" I accompanied my questing magic with another knock. "Are you home?"

Still quiet. But no, he was there. I could feel him, if barely. I heard him cough, a deep, tearing sound and stepped back from the door.

Minding my own business wasn't my best characteristic.

The door was locked, but gave way under a twist of air magic, letting me inside. The moment I passed the threshold, the scent of illness assaulted my senses, metallic and dark, a tang of early decay and old sweat hanging in the air. I coughed myself, Charlotte growling softly as her eyes shifted to wolf and back again.

Someone had pulled the shades, engulfing the room in shadow, but enough light came through the open door I could clearly see the end of Liam's bed and his long, bare feet poking out from under the covers.

"Liam." I crossed to him, anxiety taking over as I sat next to him, cradling one of his big hands in mine. Charlotte stalked to the window and threw open the shades, pouring sunlight over the room, over my friend.

I choked on a cry and touched his face even as I reached for Mom.

I need help. I felt around his power, desperate to heal him, only to feel my touch rejected.

Syd. Mom's sharp response couldn't break through my fear. *We've talked about you interrupting—*

Instead of telling her, I showed her exactly what I saw. Liam's ghostly face, veins blue beneath his transparent skin, closed eyes sunken into his head, bruise-like bags dark and terrifying. He wheezed breath out through his open mouth, lips cracked and bleeding, skin so parched from dehydration I thought he might fall apart like one of his precious books if I touched him too forcefully. He looked like he'd lost twenty pounds since I saw him earlier.

What the hell happened?

I'm on my way. Mom cut me off without another word, her own concern leaving behind a powerful aftereffect. I tried again to offer Liam healing, but nothing made it through. He'd closed himself off, shielded so tight I could barely feel him at all. But why?

What was he thinking?

Liam's eyes flickered open, but nothing of awareness lived in them. "No," he whispered. "Not you."

Um, what?

He twitched, turned from me, or tried to, as if struggling to escape. "Go away, don't want you. Go away!"

Wow. That was nice, wasn't it? No one else was here to take care of him the ungrateful—

Syd, my vampire reached for me. *Something's wrong.*

No freaking kidding. *What's going on with him?*

I don't know, she sent. *But there is magic here. Subtle. Repelling you. Repelling us.*

That makes no sense. I reached for Liam again with all of my power and finally felt what my vampire did, a slick of oily nastiness on the surface of his shields, like a film of waste. And embedded in that waste was my image.

Gross. And evidence of tampering.

Shaylee shuddered as she touched it while my demon snuffled the edges and gagged on the stench. *Sidhe*, she sent. *Glamour.*

Oh hell no. *Venner?* I was going to track his ass and beat him senseless.

I don't... she stopped. *No. Someone else.*

Lovely. I reached for Liam again only to have his body convulse, eyes bulging wide as his mouth gaped open in a silent scream of horror.

We have to break the glamour. Shaylee pushed me aside with more force than I'd ever felt from her. *If we don't, we won't be able to help him.*

I was all for that. *How?*

Just let me work. I felt her coil tight as she touched his shielding, a soft song rising from her magic. It thrummed as it grew louder, sliding across the slick surface of the repellant magic, sending ripples over its oiled surface. Liam continued to shudder, as though in some seizure, but I refused to release his hand, knowing if I did Shaylee's job would be that much harder without contact.

"Hang on, Liam," I said through teeth clenched so tight I could barely speak.

Almost there. Shaylee shuddered delicately even as she uncoiled, her magic sliding over the breaking surface of the glamour. For one disgusting moment she—we—

covered the full space around him, the filthy slime absorbed into Shaylee's energy. I instantly wanted a shower from the inside out even as her song rose in volume, her magic vibrating the repellant glamour into bits until it broke apart and vanished with one last gasp of energy.

Liam collapsed, exposed skin slick with sweat, eyes rolling into the back of his head as he wheezed for air.

Shaylee slid back into place, giving me control. *It's done,* she whispered, feeling exhausted but full of anger. *The worst kind of glamour, Syd. Thrall tied to hate.*

Liam's eyes slid forward, lids drooping, but this time when he saw me, he didn't fight. Instead, the hand I held between my own twitched ever so slightly. His lips closed, opened again, a thin sound emerging.

"Gate," he whispered as I leaned in to listen. "Gone to the green."

Charlotte's shadow hovered over me, a bottle of water, dripping condensation, thrust into my view. "He needs to drink," she said. "Now, Sydlynn."

Normally, I would have ribbed her for being bossy. Just didn't have the time. Not while I did my best to ease a few drops past Liam's parted lips, only to have him choke on the precious fluid.

Charlotte made a sound very close to a frustrated growl and shoved me aside, sliding in behind him, drawing my friend's torso up until he half-sat against her.

"Try again," she said.

Better. At least I wasn't drowning him anymore. By the time Mom rushed in with two young witches behind her, I'd managed to coax half the bottle down Liam's throat. And while I was happy we'd managed that much, he showed no signs of improvement.

Mom sank down next to me, hand on Liam's chest, her power reaching for him as mine had. A frown pulled her face out of its normal beauty as she turned to the two witches. Both appeared only a little older than me, with golden brown hair, a brother and sister from the look of them. They joined us at Liam's bedside, their joined magic sliding over Mom's.

"Syd," Mom said, holding her hand out to the pair, "this is Alphonse," the male half of the two nodded his head, gaze warm and kind. "And his sister, Lula Kennecott." The girl smiled, her power brushing the edges of mine in greeting.

Mom didn't have to tell me why there were there, or explain the soft, gentle magic they carried with them behind their matching hazel eyes.

Twins. Healers.

Awesome.

I told the two healers about the glamour and what Shaylee and I had done, glaring at Mom as I did. I stepped away and left them, not wanting to interfere, sliding down the end of the bed, keeping a loose physical grasp on Liam's foot as the two healers smiled sweetly at me before displacing Mom at his side. She stood, coming to hover over me, as the pair did their job.

Tried to. I didn't want to get in the way, but this was Liam. I couldn't just sit there. So I piggybacked, staying out of their magic flow, just in touch enough to feel how he pushed them back, too.

But wait. I'd missed it before. It wasn't Liam pushing back.

Someone else's shields surrounded him. The glamour filled two jobs, it seemed. One to keep Liam from me and the other, to prevent me from knowing what I now registered so clearly.

"Mom," I said. "Whose magic is that?"

She turned to me, frowning as the twins nodded in unison.

"He is being held," they said together, still lost in the fight to break the shielding. "Whatever power feeds these wards, it's Sidhe in nature, but doesn't originate in the patient."

I couldn't sit anymore, rising to pace, arms wrapped around me, eyes locked on Liam and the healers on the way back from the five steps to his dresser. It was hard to make the turn, head away from him, but I had to. Couldn't bear it.

What was happening to my friend?

The words he'd managed to whisper. He'd mentioned

the green.

So had Ameline's note.

Oh. My—

"We've brought down his fever." Lula's voice broke my thought and spun me around. "But he resists any healing while the shielding holds him. As if his soul is elsewhere."

Shudder. *Mom.*

She didn't acknowledge I'd spoken in her head. "Can you break through the wards?"

"We could," Alphonse said. "But he's in a fragile state, Miriam. It would do more harm than good."

"What's wrong with him?" A sick feeling rose inside me. I'd failed him when he needed me. Allowed his mother and that bastard Venner to distract me. Let Mom's warning keep me from asking questions.

"We don't know, Leader Hayle," Lula said. "He has some kind of virus. It's not natural but magical in origin. And, from what we can tell, designed to weaken his physical body and distract his mind. As for the shields… they seem to hold his body together." Lula seemed to struggle with her next words. "I fear if we break them now, Liam may not survive."

Mom twitched. *Syd*, she sent. *I'm sorry.*

So am I. Bitter, the taste of my failure. *It has to be Venner.*

Mom didn't argue. "Please, stay with him. Keep trying

to heal him of the virus."

Both twins nodded before turning back to Liam. Charlotte eased out from under my friend, coming to my side, shaking with anger.

"He feels wrong," she said. "Damaged." Her black hair shook around her, charcoaled eyes dangerously narrow. "I should have sensed it was more than a flu."

I had to clench my hands into fists to keep from hitting something as my eyes settled on a bowl and spoon next to Liam's bed. I pointed it out to Mom and the twins. "Sonja was supposed to be taking care of him," I snarled. "Said she was going to make him soup." Alphonse pounced on the bowl, a flicker of power sliding around the ceramic surface but stayed blue. He shook his head before setting it down again.

Not the soup. Why did that bring a hysterical giggle to the back of my throat? "So she's either a terrible mother," my vote, "or she's in on this with Venner," okay, also my vote.

Yeah, I got two votes. This wasn't a democracy.

"Syd," Mom said, "we still have no proof Venner or Sonja are involved. Until the twins can uncover what's wrong, we can't act."

I clenched my shaking hands, wishing I could just shake the stupid rules out of my mother. "Where are they?" Growling would get me nowhere, but I couldn't control my voice.

Mom shook all right. Her head. "If the twins uncover their involvement, I'll be the first to question them. I can't have you running off and demanding answers when we have no evidence."

She was so wrong. I still had options. "Just take care of him, Mom." I grabbed Charlotte's hand and ran for the door. "I'll be back with help."

She didn't try to stop me. Smart Mom.

I could have had Charlotte sniff Venner and Sonja down, but I wanted backup for this particular instance. And, as much as I wished I could just take the two of them out, Liam had to come first. And I had to do something. Maybe Galleytrot could find a way to heal Liam.

If anyone could.

Galleytrot? I threw the black hound's name out as a question while I took the stairs two at a time, racing for the Yard before I jumped into the veil. Charlotte didn't resist my grip, flying along beside me.

No answer. *Galleytrot.* I probed for him, let Shaylee out completely.

Nothing.

This was bad. Unless he was behind the wards of the Gate.

Deep breath, Syd.

The veil welcomed me as always, humming softly with the life of the Node, the touch of my grandmother,

Ahbi, now alive and well within it. I tried to avoid the distraction of its/her touch and it/she must have sensed something was wrong, because the usual feeling of happiness faded to grim just as I leaped out of the veil onto the side lawn of town hall back home in Wilding Springs.

The stairs took half a breath, the wards opening easily to me as I raced over and into the Sidhe Gate cavern, already calling the big dog's name.

"Galleytrot?" I stopped in the silence of the front entry, holding my breath.

"Something's wrong," Charlotte hissed, easing around me, her wolf flexing visibly inside her.

"I know." I glanced to the right, into Liam's room. Empty. And a quick look in the archive told me it was also uninhabited, at least the office space. If the hound was somewhere back in the stacks, I'd never find him.

"Sydlynn." Charlotte's humming growl caught my attention, spun me back toward the main cavern and the Gate.

Where a dark lump of fur lay sprawled on the stone.

Motionless.

chapter thirteen

A wave of panic drove a million spikes of fear through me as I threw myself over the threshold and onto my knees next to the silent body of the hound. Visions of the Wild Hunt rising without Galleytrot's vigilance, without protection for Liam, the last Gatekeeper, forced my breath from my lungs. Not to mention he was as much a part of my family as anyone. Personal feelings had a way of meaning more to me than the end of the world.

Go figure.

I plunged my hands into the fur of his face and dove inside him, Shaylee leading the way.

Galleytrot. Where was he? Not gone, please, no, not lost to us. *Galleytrot!*

Nothing. Blackness.

Silence.

Emptiness.

A flicker.

Shaylee caught onto that spark, pulled it to her, cradled it in her Sidhe magic, drawing it outward, upward. I supported her with my earth energy, my demon and vampire doing their best to offer strength while Shaylee rescued Galleytrot from the brink of death and brought him back.

He groaned softly, a rumbling noise shaking the floor as his energy slowly returned, green sparks floating from his jet-black coat. When his eyes snapped open, they flared with red fire. The great hound howled as he leaped to his feet, tossing back his head. The sound filled the room, so loud I had to clamp my hands over my ears, though it did little good. The howl wasn't just audible, but inside my head, fueled by his magic, the entire cavern rocking and shifting, dust falling from the ceiling to drift over us.

Galleytrot finally fell silent, dropping his head, panting with his long tongue lolling out of his mouth. He sank to his haunches, then his belly, drooping until his head rested in my lap, Shaylee's magic holding him close while he gathered his strength again.

I scratched his ears, kissed his muzzle, wiped at tears as I wept for what almost happened.

"Syd," he whispered. "Liam."

I hugged him. "It's all right. He's with Mom's healers at the moment. I need to know what happened."

He grumbled a growl. "You don't understand," he said. "Liam did this, Syd." One eye opened, flashing red through the sadness. "Why would he try to kill me?"

Um, what? "Tell me everything." I had to force myself to take breaths as the great hound spoke.

"He arrived home." Galleytrot panted a few times before licking his chops and continuing. "I ran to greet him, as I always do. I didn't know he intended to return."

I met Charlotte's eyes as she grunted.

Galleytrot whined like a puppy, turning his face into my lap, body limp. "Syd, he attacked me. Cut the tether of my Sidhe soul to this body."

I had no idea that was even possible. Wait, Sidhe soul? "How?"

"The power of the Gate." Galleytrot groaned softly. "I wasn't expecting him to harm me so I didn't shield against him. He just reached inside me without warning and…" the big dog chuffed, ears drooping, body shaking. "He used that power to cut the Sidhe soul inside me free. Conlaoch was so terrified, he tried to drag my mortal soul with him. And almost succeeded." Galleytrot licked the back of my hand. "If you hadn't come when you did, I don't think I would have been able to hold on much longer."

Um, confused. "Sidhe soul?" What was he talking about?

Sydlynn, Shaylee sent. *Later. This is more important.*

Okay then. "Then what happened?"

"I managed to hold on. I watched Liam open the Gate and pass through."

"Galleytrot," I said, blood running so cold, goosebumps rose all over me, "Liam is back at school. Very sick. So it wasn't him."

The dog lifted his head, met my eyes. "I wouldn't have let him through if it wasn't."

I had to talk to Mom. Whatever was wrong with Liam? Yeah, no brainer, it was tied to whoever played the imposter.

"Can you stand?" I scooted out from under him. "We have to cross the wards to talk to Mom. She needs to know about the attack." Maybe knowing Galleytrot almost died would finally snap her out of her whole "follow the rules" broken record.

And I still had to find out what the Sidhe soul stuff was about. Though, as I stood up, my brain processed Shaylee's existence.

Did Galleytrot have his own version of my Sidhe princess? And if so, why?

Galleytrot heaved himself to his feet, leaning heavily on Charlotte while Shaylee fed him power. "I must be strong enough," he said. "For Liam."

I led the pair out into the basement hall and reached for Mom, feeling Gram's mind link with me the moment I did. I told them both what we'd found, my panic rising again though I knew now Galleytrot was all right.

I had other things to panic about.

Galleytrot, you're certain it was Liam? Mom sounded as troubled as I felt.

I assure you, Miriam, the big dog sighed. *It was he.*

May we examine your memories? Gram's magic pulsed toward him. *You wanted proof, Miriam. Maybe it's in the dog's head.*

You may, Ethpeal, Galleytrot sent. *I have nothing to hide.*

I joined my mother and my grandmother. Watched Liam enter the cavern, felt our body run toward him, seen through the hound's eyes. I saw the person who looked and felt like my Sidhe friend and knew Mom and Gram did the same.

It's him, I sent. *I'd know Liam's magic anywhere.*

As would I, Galleytrot sent.

My stomach knotted as I stared at the image of Liam. *Ameline figured out how to take on a demon's form,* I sent to them. *Could she have done the same with Liam?* It made the most sense. Especially when I added her mention of seeing me on the green to his fevered muttering. What had he said?

Gone to the green.

Syd, what you're suggesting is impossible. Mom's power churned.

Actually, Gram sent, *it's not.*

You've seen this happen before, Mother? I think we both

forgot, at times, Gram used to be an Enforcer. Until she piped up with knowledge neither of us had. Made me wonder all over again what her life with the order was like.

Maybe once my life settled down, she'd find the time to tell me.

There have been instances, Gram sent. *But it requires the subject's soul.*

Ameline stole the soul of the demon boy, Todd, I sent. So it was true.

This is a little different, Syd. Gram's mental voice went silent a moment. *How much do you know about the passing of Sidhe heritage?*

It's a bloodline thing, right? I didn't have time for a history lesson.

Not exactly. Gram sighed. *Let's just say, you're not the only one with a Sidhe hitchhiker in your head.*

Shaylee muttered at that, but didn't argue.

Galleytrot's soul talk came back to me. *Sorry?*

Mother, what are you talking about? Mom sounded afraid.

It's not something that's common knowledge, Gram sent. *Not even for someone like you, Miriam.* Gram's chuckle almost made me feel better. *The only way to have Sidhe blood is to have one reincarnate inside you.*

I already knew that was what happened with Shaylee and me. But I had no idea it was common practice. Now the big hound's talk of his Sidhe soul was beginning to make sense.

What? Mom's shock came through the connection so clearly I could see her standing outside Liam's room with her mouth hanging open. Just a flash of image, but enough. *Sidhe power is parasitical?*

Shaylee didn't like her tone or terminology one bit. She tried to send a shaft of Sidhe fire back toward my mother, only to shut down because I kind of loved the witch on the other end, thanks and wanted to keep her around a while.

Not parasites, exactly, Gram sent. *But co-inhabitors. Most witches don't even know they have Sidhe souls inside them. Only the strongest are able to influence or even contact their host.*

Okay then. *Hang on,* I sent. *How do they get here? The Sidhe realm is sealed.*

From ordinary magic, Gram sent. *And there are more Gates than just ours, Syd. It's part of a Gatekeeper's job to sort souls.*

Shudder. I was actually kind of glad Liam never mentioned that. *So you're saying Ameline stole the reincarnated soul of a Sidhe?*

Not just any soul, she sent. *But the one inhabiting Liam. The one his father, his grandfather, all of his ancestors carried for centuries. Divided between them until only one Gatekeeper remained.*

Liam.

Gram went on. *The hound can tell you more, but that's the basic gist.*

So Ameline is using this soul to take the shape of who she wants to mimic? I shook my head, trying to wrap my mind around it. *Why doesn't she look like the Sidhe soul?* And what had she done to herself to eliminate her scent? What was she becoming?

Because she's on this plane, Gram sent. *The mechanics are a little complicated, ruled by plane law. But once she crossed over through the Gate, you can bet she took on the shape of the Sidhe himself.*

And if a reincarnated soul is taken from a host? My heart went to Liam.

It's no wonder the boy is sick, Gram's mental voice grated. *And if we don't retrieve the soul and return it to him, he'll die.*

There's no way Ameline managed this herself. My power surged, whipping into a frenzy. Anger was my favorite go-to when I felt helpless and this was a perfect example. *Venner had to have helped her.*

Mom didn't protest.

Smart Mom.

I'm going after her. I spun toward the entrance, only to have Charlotte block my path while Gram and Mom both latched onto me with power.

Not alone you're not.

You get back here right now, young lady!

Guess whose mind said what.

Ameline is on the Sidhe side, I sent while I squirmed to pull free of their power, glaring at Charlotte. *With Liam's soul! You just said he'll die without it!*

And running off without back up and no intel will get you dead. Gram's grunt actually made me pause. *Your days of running off half-cocked have to stop, girl. Time to work smarter, not harder.*

Sucked. So. Much.

But she was right.

Mom, how is he? Maybe if we brought him to the Gate cavern, the power of the place would help him.

She didn't say anything for a moment, probably conferring with the twins. When she finally reached for me, her tone was grim. *Not well*, she sent. *But stable.*

Can we bring him here? A quick trip through the veil—

Forgive me for interrupting, Lula's mental voice was as gentle as her spoken one, *but moving him now would be a mistake. We will consider it as a last resort. But in his weakened condition, I fear we could do more harm than good.*

There went that idea. *Fine, I'm coming back.* I spun, eyes locked on Galleytrot.

"I'm coming with you," he growled, eyes flaring red.

"We can't leave the Gate unprotected." This idea wasn't working out so well, either.

"With Venemeth in your mother's sights and Ameline on the other side, I must make Liam my priority. He is our only hope to keep control of the Gate. Now that she has his Sidhe soul, restoring Liam is more important than the portal itself."

I wasn't sure I agreed with him, but we had to do something.

"Seal the Gate itself," the hound said. "She might be able to open it, but if you shield the inside, it will take her some time to break through and escape." He turned to the entry. "I'll reinforce the wards at the entry so none may pass within or without. That should be sufficient for the time it will take for me to examine Liam myself."

It wasn't the best-case scenario, but we were kind of low on good ideas. It didn't take Shaylee long to form a thin but powerful seal around the outside edge of the Gate. While Ameline could activate the door itself, the ward would act like a doorstop, keeping it from opening.

I stepped out into the musty basement and offered Galleytrot power as he took his turn, green magic pouring into the existing shields until the glow solidified into shining glass only one with Sidhe blood could see.

Mom, I sent, as comfortable with our solution as I could be. *We're on our way. And I'm bringing Galleytrot with me.*

As hard as it was to leave the Gate behind, knowing now full well Ameline was already on the other side and having done everything I possibly could to ensure the Gate's safety I gathered up the hound and my bodywere and dove into the veil for Harvard before I could change my mind.

chapter fourteen

Galleytrot chuffed unhappily over Liam while I paced the room again and tried to stay out of his way both magically and physically. The Kennecott twins stepped aside the moment the giant black hound entered the room, hovering together in the corner where I occasionally brushed Alphonse's robe with a muttered apology.

"We've done what we can." Lula met my eyes as I turned for another pass. Her concern shone out of her pale face, freckles standing out in perfect little brown circles across her cheeks. Hazel eyes that reminded me of Liam's showed more empathy than I was prepared to deal with.

"Thank you." I stopped long enough to reach for them both with my energy, to express my gratitude for their help the best way I knew how. The twins linked with me without hesitation, the brother as kindly as his sister.

If you ever need our help, Coven Leader, Lula said, *Alphonse and I are both at your service.*

Her brother wrinkled his nose. *Call me Phon. Please. I beg you.*

I almost laughed. *What family?* I'd never met them before despite the fact they looked about my age.

None, they sent together. *We were raised by the Council and the Enforcer order, but we've remained autonomous.*

Well now, how interesting was that? *Any reason why?*

They shrugged in unison, their power tied together as much as their physical bond and I found myself thinking about the Lawrence sisters. Except there was nothing creepy about Lula and Phon.

We haven't found a family we trust enough to pledge our magic. Lula slid her hand into her brother's. *Neither of us cares for politics.*

Growing up raised by the Council? I could hardly blame them.

Well, thank you. I turned back to Liam, hearing Galleytrot groan softly as he sank to his haunches next to the bed, turning his big head to meet my eyes, red fire glowing deep within. *I have no doubt the two of you kept Liam going.* Galleytrot's slow headshake dropped my stomach to my toes. *And I might have to ask you to keep it up, if you're willing.*

They nodded immediately. *Our pleasure*, they sent,

bowing their heads to me.

I left them with a final burst of gratitude from my power before sitting on the edge of the bed next to Galleytrot. My fingers found the thick fur around his left ear and dug in as I focused on my sick friend. He looked better, at least physically. Whatever the twins managed, they stabilized his body. But I could tell from the sadness and anger rumbling deep inside the great hound they'd been unable to restore the part of him which made Liam whole.

Still, I had to ask. "How is he, Galleytrot?" I looked up as he answered, eyes drawn to the door and the sound of murmured conversation as Mom waved off a pair of Enforcers in black robes before coming back inside on quiet feet. I gestured for her to join us.

"It is as you feared," Galleytrot said. I heard Gram sigh in my head, her connection to me as strong as ever. "The Sidhe soul he once carried has been stripped from him."

"How?" Surely the connection he had with his Sidhe was as strong as the one I had with Shaylee. Considering he'd been born that way and was now the Gatekeeper. I knew my princess ego would fight to the death before she'd let anyone strip her from me.

Shaylee's firm agreement was all the reassurance I needed I was right.

"The virus," Galleytrot said. "It's weakened not only

his body, but his mind, muddled his thoughts. Because of this, his Sidhe would have been equally as vulnerable."

Ripe for the picking. "What's the Sidhe's name?" Now that I knew the soul was his own person, it seemed important information.

"Cian," Galleytrot said. "The creator of the Gate."

"Hang on," I said. "I thought the maji made the gates."

"The barrier between planes was created by the maji," the hound said. "But the Gates were built by the Sidhe. Each Gate by one builder, whose soul is carried by the Gatekeepers."

That's why all the O'Dane men look alike, Gram sent to us. *They are literally the same person, thanks to Cian's influence and the pressure of the Gate.*

"So when Ameline went over..." my heart clenched.

She still looked like Liam, Gram sent, finishing my sentence. *Like Cian the builder.*

"Will Liam survive if the soul is not returned?" Mom was being practical, I knew that, but it didn't keep my fury from forming a pulsing knot in my lower back.

"He may." Galleytrot gently licked Liam's hand. "But I doubt it, Miriam. He was born to bear Cian's soul. And with all of the Gatekeepers of his line but him gone, at least from this plane, Liam is the only carrier here. Unlike Sydlynn," he looked up to meet my eyes, "who is used to having Shaylee's full soul, Liam spent most of his life sharing it. When he took on his father's portion after he was killed, Liam grew stronger in the power of the Sidhe. And with Fergus's near death, forced to retreat to the Sidhe realm, he left a further portion behind for his grandson."

"To which his body adapted." Mom nodded. "And now that it's gone..."

"I'm certain Syd can tell you just how painful it can be to go without a part of herself." I hugged the dog while Mom grimaced.

"I know the feeling myself," she said as my mind flickered to Batsheva Moromond and Mom being stripped of the family magic. It felt like a century ago. "But we both survived."

"Because you're witches," Galleytrot said. "Your bodies are infused with magic, no matter what's taken or blocked from you. Liam's body is human without the magic of his Sidhe soul. It spent his entire life infusing him with its power. Now it's gone, his human form can't support itself any longer."

"Like an addiction?" I tried to wrap my head around it.

"In a way. But worse, because it's not something from which he will recover. Every cell in his body will collapse eventually without the Sidhe magic to support him."

"What about other magic?" Mom's voice was steady, but the hand stroking Liam's hair out of his face shook

113

just a bit. "Can we shore up his physical form with earth power?"

Galleytrot shrugged, wet nose drooping as he bowed his head. "I've been trying," he whispered. "Am I succeeding? I have no idea."

"Okay," I said, sitting back, crossing my arms over my chest in absolute refusal to accept any of this was going to stop me. "So as far as we know, Ameline has taken another soul against its will and crossed over to the Sidhe realm. But why?" I hated her so much in that moment I could barely speak. "What is she after this time?"

And why did she bother to warn me? Why did she want me to know—some sick sense of humor? Taunting me?

I'd have thought she'd learned her lesson on Demonicon. But she'd had a goal in mind when she lured me to my grandmother's dying side.

Did she have a further goal now?

Galleytrot grumbled a low growl, the distant sound of a thunderclap in his displeasure. "If I'm to understand correctly," he said, "she is attempting to become maji. And to do that, she needs all the powers of the realms. Sidhe, demon, witch."

"And a few more," I said.

"She failed on Demonicon because she had stolen a soul." Galleytrot pawed the hardwood floor, nails clicking over the varnish. "No demon would willingly give up their power, however. Correct?"

My demon roared her agreement. "Yeah, that's a safe bet," I said.

"I'm afraid that's not the case for the Sidhe," he said. "There are those souls still trapped in spirit form in the realm who would willingly join her just to exist again."

"So all she really needed was to cross," I said, my tension driving my right knee to jiggle at a rapid pace. "She can then dump Liam's stolen Sidhe soul and take on one more willing to help her out." Lovely. Just. Freaking. Lovely.

Why didn't it feel quite right?

"It's not that simple," Galleytrot said. "She would need permission from Her Majesty. As would the soul looking to be reborn."

"But there's nothing to keep the Seelie Queen from saying yes, is there?" I heard Shaylee sigh in my mind.

My mother would do so if she knew it would cause mischief, my Sidhe princess agreed. *But I think I see a flaw in Ameline's plan.*

I opened my mind to Mom, Galleytrot and Gram, who remained oddly silent through the whole conversation. *Go ahead, Shaylee,* I sent. *What is Ameline missing?*

She doesn't need just any soul. Shaylee paused and I could feel her consciousness working out what she wanted to say. *You are my equal. As is your demon. And vampire. We all share your body. We aren't just guests.*

That gave me the creeps for a minute, but I agreed. My demon had taken me over enough times back when I still rejected my magic I believed it. And Shaylee was a Sidhe princess after all. Considering the vampire inside me was the mother of all undead...

So you're saying Ameline can't just help herself to any Sidhe soul, I sent. *She needs one that's her equal.*

I believe so, Shaylee sent.

There aren't many, Galleytrot rumbled. *As much as I hate to admit it, Ameline's power, her witch magic, is probably as strong as Syd's.* Oh no he did *not* just say that. *Which means to find an equal, she will need someone similar to Shaylee. The Queen, for example. Shaylee herself. Perhaps Thalion.*

What about Cian? He was the creator of the Gate, after all. Why wasn't he powerful enough for her?

Cian is a strong soul, Galleytrot sent. *But there is a reason he was a Gate creator and not in the ruling class. His power was sufficient to create the Gate, now fed by all the magic of the Sidhe realm as it pours through the veil between planes. But that was the extent of his ability. And after so many years being diffused through O'Danes, having his own magic supplanted after the Gate's creation by the magic of the realm, Cian just isn't strong enough to be considered her equal.*

But the other two you mentioned are still alive, Gram finally spoke up, voice a whip-crack of irritation. *And if she kills them for their souls, it's not likely they'll go along willingly.*

As much as Prince Thalion kind of pissed me off the last time we met, I didn't wish death on him. Or an eternity with Ameline for company. *What about the Unseelie?*

Galleytrot's mental snarl was punctuated with the sound of a rockslide. *Yes*, he sent. *Possible. There are a few Unseelie souls lurking who might fit the job.*

And Liam's soul? I hugged myself as I stared down at my friend. He never mentioned Cian talked to him, if he even did.

Made me wonder if there was communication between the two and Liam never mentioned it, what else had he kept from me?

If she finds one strong enough, Galleytrot sent, *she can merely dump Cian and leave him behind.*

Stranding Liam on our side of the Gate without his Sidhe soul.

I love him, Syd, Galleytrot sent. *But Liam's loss is bigger than how we feel. Without him, the Gate is unprotected.*

Which meant we were right back to where we started with the whole Gatekeeper problem. And I was left with a single solution.

Bracing myself for the fight I knew was coming, I touched all of their minds with as much conviction and confidence as I could muster.

There's no other choice, I sent. *I have to go after her.*

CHAPTER FIFTEEN

The landslide of objections I was expecting didn't come. Not that Mom and Gram didn't try.

Absolutely not, young lady.

You've lost your fool mind, girl.

I loved them so much. Predictable. But neither sounded convinced by their own denial.

We can't let the Gate go unprotected, I sent, aiming for cool and logical, knowing that would win Mom over. *Liam is absolutely necessary and we all know it.*

My mother hesitated, but Gram barreled through anyway. *You have no idea what you're getting yourself into*, she snapped. *The Sidhe realm isn't some walk in the park.*

I realize that, I sent back, but she wasn't done.

No, she shot at me, words arrows of anger. *You don't. You've only had a taste of what waits on the other side. There's nothing real there. Nothing. It's all illusion built on lies and deceit,*

118

all for the Queen's pleasure. Wow, Gram wasn't fooling around. The more she talked, the pissier she got. *Aoilainn ap Danaan might be Shaylee's mother, but she only has her own interests at heart.*

Shaylee didn't argue. Not a good sign.

So what do you suggest we do, Gram? I hated to throw it back at her, but I was done sitting around and not getting involved. Trouble or no trouble, Liam was my friend and Ameline the biggest menace since the Brotherhood.

Ameline, a maji? Shudder.

Gram's pause told me volumes. *This is the stupidest idea I've ever heard*, she finally snapped.

Nice to hear I have your confidence, I sent, words sarcastic, but mental tone gentle. *If there was another way, Gram, I'd be the first one to take it.*

Liar. She grumbled another moment. *You can't go alone.*

Agreed. Mom's hand reached for mine.

She won't be, Shaylee sent just as Galleytrot hummed low in his chest.

Neither of them will be, he sent.

There, see? Bright and sparkly wasn't cutting it, but I'd committed now and couldn't stop, no matter how lame. *I have a Sidhe princess and a hound of the Wild Hunt beside me. What could go wrong?*

Gram snorted a laugh without humor in it. *This is a disaster.*

It is. Galleytrot leaned against me. *I'm sorry, Syd. But*

Ethpeal is correct. This will end badly.

Way to make me feel better. *Here's the plan*, I sent. *We go to the Gate and call Thalion.* The idea of seeing him again made Shaylee feel sad. I guess I understood since he was in love with her while she still pined for her sleeping love, Gwynn ap Nudd, buried with the Wild Hunt under my backyard. I wasn't sure how I felt about her loving a guy who sent her to her death, but it was her heart, not mine, and who was I to judge? *We tell him about Ameline and ask him to warn the Queen.* I knew things would go further than that, but if I convinced Mom and Gram, I could at least act when I had to without too much guilt.

And if he turns you down? Way to ruin my plan, Gram.

Then we have to cross, I sent, firm and decisive. *There is no other alternative.*

You're forgetting Fergus O'Dane, Gram sent. *If Ameline does release Cian, he won't be homeless. He'd return to the one person in the Sidhe realm with whom he has a connection.*

That made me feel a little better. *So we contact Fergus too*, I sent. And hope he had a way to help beyond moral support.

I think you give Ameline too much credit, my vampire spoke up. *When has she ever willingly released power unless it meant her own survival?*

You think she'll keep Cian even while she takes on another soul? Was that even possible?

Um, Syd? Count your egos, sister.

Right.

I'm sending an Enforcer with you. Mom released my hand.

You can't, I sent back. *Mom, a witch Enforcer will be vulnerable in the Sidhe realm without a soul.* Not blood, as I'd been taught but now knew to be false. Wow, I actually listened in class, even if it was the wrong information.

Wicked.

Someone strong in earth magic should be all right for a short time, Galleytrot sent. *And having a warrior with us might make Aoilainn pay attention. There are certain games she enjoys when others approach her, and sending a suitable party to satisfy her sense of arrogance could mean the difference between her receiving us or our summary expulsion.*

He turned and chuffed at Charlotte who cocked her head to one side, eyes meeting his. After a short, private moment, she bobbed her head.

Charlotte will come too, Galleytrot sent. *She will be the second hound. Which gives us a princess, a knight and two hounds. But we could still use an elder.*

You leave that to me. Gram's magic rippled toward me. *I'll meet you at the Gate.*

Mother. Mom's panic was as real as mine. *You can't both go. You'll be leaving the coven open and at risk.*

There are no promises any of us will return if we are forced to cross, Galleytrot sent. *Ethpeal, we should use another.*

To hell with you all, Gram snarled. *I was an Enforcer. And I've had direct dealings with Her Royal Pain In The Assness. So*

I'm going. No more arguments.

Mom, I reached for her, my turn to take her hand. *I want Quaid. No question.*

He's not fully trained. I felt her fret, but knew she agreed with me. And yet.

He knows me. And I know him. Intimately. Blushing. *Our power fits seamlessly together. Another Enforcer would just get in my way.*

Mom nodded quickly, eyes going distant as she left us a moment to send a mental command. I turned to Galleytrot who laid his great head on the bed, eyes blinking slowly as he stared at silent Liam.

"How much damage is being done and how quickly?" I took Liam's cold hand in mine, feeling how thin his skin had become, how shrunken his form.

"I don't know," Galleytrot groaned. "There is no way of knowing." His big head lifted as he licked his chops. "While I know this is secondary to saving him, we need to find Sonja. And Venner."

I met Mom's eyes as she returned to the conversation. Her jaw clamped tight, gaze narrowing, but I knew her anger wasn't aimed at me this time.

"Lord Venemeth has outstayed his welcome," Mom said. "I've already triggered the watching Enforcers to tighten the leash."

Magic whooshed in the air, two black-robed figures appearing in the middle of the room with barely enough space to spare. I looked up, met Quaid's eyes, felt his power slide around me even as Pender Tremere, the tall, lean leader of the Enforcer Order, scowled at Mom.

"You can't be serious," he said. "Miriam, Quaid might be my best trainee, but he's not ready for a solo mission."

I stood and reached for Quaid's hand, feeling all of my magic respond to him as our energy met before opening up to Pender to let him feel us together. The man's eyes widened before his shoulders sagged.

"Sir," Quaid said. "Permission to take the assignment."

Pender nodded slowly. "I had no idea you two were bound," he said. "Granted."

Hmmm. What?

I didn't get to ask what Pender meant. Nor did I care at the moment. Likely it had something to do with the stupid promise Mom made Batsheva when Quaid and I were babies, betrothing us to each other.

Yeah. That turned out well.

No time for regrets in the love department. I motioned for the twins to join us and turned to Liam. "Please do what you can," I said. "He needs as much earth support as possible."

They both nodded, taking Mom's place as Galleytrot stood and backed up until he leaned against my hip, Charlotte standing close behind me.

"First things first," Galleytrot growled. "I have to talk

to Sonja and find out what Venner knows. Maybe there is something I'm missing." Mom's mind flashed the location, one of the senior housing apartments off campus. At least she'd been smart enough to keep Venner away from the students directly.

"Good idea." I saluted Mom and Pender. "Warn your Enforcers we're coming," I said as I tore a hole in the veil, not even waiting to leave to do it. The Enforcer leader's arrival made me bold and Mom didn't protest. "You might want to be right behind us so nothing regrettable happens."

I personally hoped they were late as I dove into the tear between planes, pulling my three companions along with me.

chapter sixteen

I was actually a little surprised to step out of the veil in Venner's quarters and find him waiting for me, nasty Unseelie smirk on his face. Honestly, I expected he already ran, figured out a way to deflect the Enforcers, forcing me to waste precious time hunting him down and wringing his scrawny Fey neck.

Galleytrot's rumbling fury echoed toward the vaulted ceiling, partially collapsing Venner's smile. My eyes scanned the room, found Sonja sitting in a Victorian chair, Spaft near the door. I didn't have to tell her to act, Charlotte already stalking the tall, skinny woman, blocking her exit.

"Your little charade is over, Venner," I said as Quaid's power rippled through the room, a blue glow sealing off the two large bay windows of the sitting room as well as the white door with the shining glass knob, sending rainbow sparkles onto the floor.

"Really, Your Highness," Venner said, bringing his drink to his lips with a casual pinky raise. "Whatever are you talking about?"

"Was it your plan to kill Liam?" I couldn't hold my temper back any longer, not while he treated my friend's decline with so much disdain. "Or just leave him a vegetable?"

Venner's brows came together ever so slightly. "Liam is fine," he said. "I just spoke with him this afternoon."

Sonja twitched slightly, hands fluttering in her lap. "Liam?" She blinked, as though waking from a dream. "What's wrong with Liam?"

Everything froze inside me—my heart, my blood, my breath. I felt for the Unseelie soul inside Liam's mother and knew, even as I cursed myself, Ameline tricked me again.

"Sonja," I said, "did you stop by to make Liam soup after class?" I already knew the answer. Saw her face crumple as she pressed one shaking hand to her lips.

"Today?" She looked up, met my eyes. "Is my baby sick?"

Ameline. Galleytrot's howl in my head hurt so much I had to clench my fists and my jaw to keep from crying out.

The soul inside Sonja shuddered, weak and lazy, her body heavy with a sense of exhaustion I'd also felt in

Liam. My stomach did a slow back flip at my understanding. Ameline had taken Sonja's Sidhe soul and used it to appear as Liam's mother. That's why, when I saw Sonja with Liam, she hadn't seemed afraid of me any longer. Was confident enough to sweep him away from me. Liam's soul wasn't the only one Ameline tapped into. But she must have known Venner would be watching Liam's mother.

How had he missed it? Unless he knew she'd planned it all along.

"Liam's Sidhe soul is missing," I said, blunt and harsh, not caring if it hurt Sonja, furious with her as much as with Ameline, for allowing Venner to influence her. Angry. Just angry.

Venner's frown turned to a scowl as he flowed to his feet. "What?" His eyes drifted to Sonja. "What have you done, fool woman?"

I pushed myself into his space before he could reach for her, poking him sharply in the chest with one index finger, power behind it. "Don't blame her, you jackass," I snarled. "Who gave Ameline access to Liam in the first place?"

Venner's pale complexion turned positively ashen. "No," he whispered, sinking into his chair. "This isn't how it was supposed to happen."

I caught a flicker of motion out of the corner of my eye as Spaft shifted position, but ignored her, knowing

Charlotte wouldn't let the woman get away even if she managed to make it past Quaid's shielding. "So this was your idea," I said. "Spill it, Venner. What's Ameline's plan?"

I already knew. But I needed him to confess in front of witnesses. To cover my ass and Mom's. Damned politics.

Venner fixed me with a look filled with fury and broken hope. "I need to find her," he said. "Has she crossed already?"

"Just answer the damned question," I said.

Venner's hands quivered around his glass as he clutched it in front of him, eyes locked on the slowly sloshing amber liquid inside. "I was merely going to borrow the boy's power," he said. "Only to allow me to cross, that is all."

"What was Ameline's role in all this?" How much of an idiot was he, anyway?

"It was her suggestion we use Liam," Venner said, shaking his head, green eyes flashing with Sidhe fire. "I'm a fool."

Duh. "Go on."

"She said she needed a soul, that was all." Venner lurched to his feet, some of his natural grace gone as he paced toward the window while Galleytrot tracked him step by step. When Venner turned, sparks in his gaze shone from the shadow of his form where the streaming sun cast him in darkness. "I agreed to help her acquire one."

Wheels turned. "Is that why you were poking and prodding the students during your lecture?"

He sagged further. "We were examining other souls, to see if any had the strength of Liam's. So we could remain under your radar." Venner's body twitched. "The virus was her idea. I had no idea she'd already implemented it."

"She did," I said. "Obviously, Ameline had no interest in keeping you in the loop." Jackass. "Did you know she took Sonja's soul?"

His eyes darkened as his face fell. "The first time," he said.

Liam's mother gasped, a hand to her throat. Whatever, lady.

"The first time." Calm, Syd. Patience. Wringing his neck won't get you answers.

Venner was silent a moment. "We had to test it. To make sure the disguise would work." He met my eyes again. "And it did. Liam was completely deceived. Ameline used her power to begin the process with Liam, implanting the suggestion he avoid you so we could work without your interference."

Sick bastard. "Kind of backfired on you, didn't it?"

"She told me she knew how to disguise me once the virus did its job." He shook his head, long hair flowing in its twin silver clasps. "That she could help me use Liam's magic to appear like him, so the Gate would let me pass without alerting the Sidhe I'd returned if we couldn't find another more suitable soul."

"Instead she duped you," I said. "She tricked you into trusting her so she could have access to Sonja for the second time. Easier once the soul was used to Ameline, I imagine. Made it simple for her to steal Liam's mother's form and strip him herself."

Venner took a step toward me, features clear again as he left the backlight of the bright window. Real anguish touched his face, though for all I knew he'd been practicing. And real to a Sidhe? Who knew what that was.

Shaylee huffed her irritation at my cynicism, even though it wasn't aimed at her directly, as Venner spoke.

"It was never meant to be permanent," he said. "I was going to return the soul to the boy after I passed through."

Good to know the soul could be returned. And since Sonja was still in possession of hers, I had hope for Liam's recovery.

"Sure you were," I said.

Venner shrugged. "The moment I released it upon crossing, the soul of Cian would have simply returned to Liam on his own."

I pictured a green-tinted rubber band snapping the Gate creator's Sidhe mist back to Liam with cartoonish impact.

What was wrong with me? This was no laughing matter.

Sonja's dazed expression was long gone, destroyed, I supposed, by Venner's confession. She surged to her feet, tears coursing down her face, hate trembling through her entire body as the glamour he'd held her under shattered and fell away.

"What have you done?" She lunged at him, throwing herself on the Unseelie lordling, tearing at his clothing as she shrieked her rage. Quaid took two steps forward, arms around her, magic wrapping her in a cocoon as he pulled her back, still fighting. She finally sagged in Quaid's control, bursting into tears. "I believed in you, in your lies. Where's our new life, my life of peace with Liam? What have you done to my son?"

She clearly missed the whole part where Ameline used her to get to Liam. That I'd been fooled by the act. But Ameline's depiction was different enough, I knew it was Sonja who first appeared at my dorm door, not my evil witch nemesis.

Though I wouldn't put it past the evil witch to come see me just to test out her new form.

Laughing at me all the while.

I wanted to kill her and bring her back to life just so I could kill her again.

Charlotte's growl alerted me and I spotted Spaft

easing closer to the door. I wasn't sure what the hideous woman expected. But escape wasn't even a remote option. Still, I'd underestimated too many people in the past to let her get the jump on me.

"What was your role in all this, Hortense?" I prodded her with earth magic, making her scowl, skin pulled in tight lines by the impossibly perfect bun at the base of her neck.

"Just a pawn in another game," she said, as Venner's glass shattered. I glanced over my shoulder, saw the shining shards scattered at his feet, a terrible expression of rage on his face.

"What did she promise you, evil one?" Venner's normally musical voice grated across my eardrums, the thrum of heaving earth beneath it. "What did Ameline promise you to betray me and our plans to go home?"

Her black eyes narrowed, light flashing on the lenses of her glasses. "Your plans," she spit. "Your goals. It was always about you, wasn't it, my lord?" She shook a little, whole body trembling. "I have served you faithfully for years. And you plan to abandon me?" One of her hands fisted, punching her own thigh as her anger escaped. "And you accuse me of betrayal?"

He stared at her, a flash of shock crossing his face. "You fool," he said. "You could never have crossed over with me. You know that. Your Sidhe soul isn't strong enough to protect you for prolonged periods of time.

You would fall victim to the glamour of the realm."

Spaft didn't say anything more, back straight, chin up, still shaking. Venner cursed, a soft sound, but a word so vile in Sidhe Shaylee winced. I was kind of glad she didn't offer a translation.

"It was Hortense who introduced me to Miss Benoit," Venner said. "She was our liaison."

Interesting. I couldn't help the nasty smile that crossed my lips. "Conspiring with a wanted witch will get you arrested, Ms. Spaft." She just glared back, one hand rising to adjust her glasses. "But I have to say, I didn't take you for a self-starter. So, what was it Ameline offered you?" I already had a good idea, especially after her little speech to Venner, but I wanted—needed—her to say it. "Power? Money? A better first name?"

Spaft snarled at me, black eyes snapping, her hideous face shining with hate. "What he never offered me," she spat. "Not this weak incarnation I carry, but the soul of a full Unseelie Lady. And my proper place at court."

Venner shook his head, hands in the pockets of his tailored suit-pants, looking like a super model ready for the runway while his power flashed in his eyes and sent sparks from the ends of his shining silver hair. "She lied to you," he said. "Ameline would never offer you what you can't have. No Sidhe would willingly incarnate in you." Now he was just being cruel. But she flinched from every word as though he lashed her with them. "You aren't worthy of the pathetic soul you already carry." He turned from her, face a stone mask of beauty. "And because of your duplicity, I will personally see to it you never acquire what you're looking for."

Spaft sagged, a howl of anger and sadness escaping her lips. But despite her anguish, somehow, I didn't think she was all that repentant.

CHAPTER SEVENTEEN

Mom didn't waste time showing up. We'd just wrangled the confession from Spaft when the seal Quaid made shuddered and parted, the door to the sitting room opening to admit Mom and Pender, three Enforcers at their backs, the scowling board of governors trailing behind them.

"Really, Miriam," Gertrude's gravel voice made me want to buy her some lozenges, "what is the meaning of this?" She smiled and offered a little wave to Venner before fixing Mom with her baleful beady eyes again. "I thought we told you Lord Venemeth has our full support?"

I could tell from the tightness around Mom's eyes she was this close to dropkicking the nasty old woman out one of the windows. I almost wished she would.

Popcorn, please. The show was about to start.

"Lord Venner has some explaining to do," Mom said. Nodded to me. *Did he confess?*

He sure did. I motioned to Venner. "Your precious Sidhe lord here planned to strip the soul from the Wilding Springs Gatekeeper in order to return to his own plane."

Gertrude sniffed while Elegance shifted her position, head brushing the hanging light fixture. "You say 'planned'," she said. "If he hasn't done so yet, there is nothing to prosecute. We have only your word as evidence, and that certainly isn't enough." She seemed rather satisfied by that. As did Gertrude and Periwinkle.

"The only problem?" I wanted to knock their fool heads together. "Thanks to him, another beat him to it. Liam O'Dane has had his Sidhe soul stolen and now lies on his deathbed." Okay, we weren't sure he would die. But it was likely enough I didn't feel like I stretched the truth too far.

They finally looked uncomfortable, though Gertrude stuck out her chin in a stubborn jut. "Sidhe business," she said. "And has nothing to do with us."

Was she serious. Really? I met Mom's eyes with my mouth hanging open while my mother ground her teeth together.

You see now, she sent. *What I deal with.*

Oh. My. Swearword.

"Listen up," I snapped. "You might not think this is your problem, but you're very wrong. Not only is the

Gate no longer protected by a Gatekeeper, leaving all of our plane open to Sidhe magic should the knock go unanswered, but Venner's little plan failed to a witch." I watched the three flinch. Yeah, that's right, ladies. Stuff that in your ugly craws and choke on it. "And not just any witch, but witchdom's most wanted—Ameline Benoit."

Had their attention at last. "It's not true, is it, my lord?" Gertrude's plea was a parody of grief coming from her mouth.

Venner spread his hands, a showman to the end as he smiled sadly at her. "I was duped, Gertie," he said.

Lying bastard.

She nodded, patted at the corner of her eyes, shining with tears while her two companions did the same.

"Be that as it may," she said, "if you were involved with a witch who has broken our laws, our hands are tied." Elegance blew her nose on a dainty hanky, the honking sound forcing me to bite my lips to keep from grinning. If they had any idea how ridiculous they were...

"You agree then," Mom said at her most mild, a sign she was ready to lose her cool. "Lord Venemeth is now a criminal under our laws?"

Periwinkle nodded. "Of course," she said. "Gertrude, we must act."

Gertrude sighed, but gestured to Mom. "Do your job then, Miriam, what are you waiting for? Take this criminal into custody and have him questioned."

"He didn't act alone." I pointed at Ms. Spaft. "Under his own admission, and her confession, she was the one who had the first contact with Ameline."

Gertrude sniffed at me like I'd spoken out of turn, but nodded. "Very well."

No "well done, Coven Leader Hayle." No "you've saved the day, Sydlynn." Nope. The three of them just spun and left, marching out as though they were the heroines of the hour, leaving Mom to sigh and run her hand over her eyes before straightening and addressing Pender.

"Enforcer Leader," she said. "If you would?"

"Please," Sonja practically fell on Mom before anyone could stop her. "Where is my Liam?"

Mom's eyes met mine as she waved off the Enforcers. "He's in good hands," she said before gesturing for one of the Enforcers to take Sonja. "I'll make sure that remains the case until he can be restored."

Sonja was led from the room, sobbing openly, pausing in her weeping only long enough to lunge at Spaft. Whether it was a good thing or not, the Enforcer guard held them apart. I would have liked to see what Sonja could have done with a few good blows.

As for Spaft, she just slumped in the guard's arms and left without a word. Maybe she was finally realizing the deal she made with the devil fell apart on her. Surely she wasn't regretting what she'd done, but only that she'd been caught.

But when the Enforcers came for Venner, he locked gazes with me, his magic reaching out. "You must take me with you." So much desperation. Pathetic, really.

"Yeah, that's going to happen." I cut off his magic's reach and slammed some of mine into his chest, sending him back a step. "You've proven yourself oh so trustworthy in the past, Venner."

"You don't understand," he said. "You'll need me, Your Highness."

Shaylee shifted inside me while I stared Venner down. "I'm going to open the Gate and talk to Thalion," I said. "That's it." Right, Syd. Don't bluff a bluffer.

Venner's green eyes never left mine as the guards tried to lead him away. "You know you'll be forced to cross," he said, pulling against the Enforcers. "And there is no promise Ameline went to the Seelie court for help, is there?"

Hang on a second. "Wait." I knew I'd regret it, saw the doubt flash over Mom's face, but had to hear him out. Damn him. "What are you talking about?" I already knew. Hadn't we just talked about this possibility?

"Ameline asked me about my court," Venner said, speaking fast, face open and pleading. "And if you intend to enter the Unseelie lands, you will have to have me with you. Or my king will kill you before you make it three paces into his territory."

I knew the moment Galleytrot rumbled his unhappiness, the floor shaking slightly beneath my feet from the pressure of his displeasure, Venner wasn't lying.

Craptastic.

Oh, come on, I sent to the big dog. *Are you serious?*

I hadn't even considered this, he sent. *I'm sorry, Syd. But he's right. Queen Aoilainn might be tricky and up to no good, but King Odhran can be downright nasty. And if you enter his realm without permission or a guide, it's possible he won't even listen. Shaylee is his enemy's daughter, remember? And Cian is Seelie as well.*

Lovely. There has to be another way.

There isn't. Gram's words cut across my mind. *Just bring the damned fool with you.*

Galleytrot shook his whole body, fur throwing green sparks. *I'll tether him with the magic of the Wild Hunt*, he sent. *But there are no guarantees, if we pass into the Sidhe realm, my hold will be sufficient.*

I turned to Mom and saw the doubt already on her face.

"Syd," she said. Sighed. "I know better than to argue with you. But you realize, now that Venner has been declared a criminal, by liberating him to take him with you, you could be charged with aiding in his escape."

Beat my head against a brick wall. "Shut. Up."

Mom shrugged. Rubbed her temples. "We'll figure it out," she said. "Just get him out of here before something happens."

Venner's beaming smile did nothing for my temper, not even when he flinched as Galleytrot's magic whipped out and grabbed him in a fist of green energy. Venner staggered ever so slightly before nodding once to the giant hound.

I couldn't help but worry we'd just played right into Ameline's hands somehow. And if Venner had any plans to double-cross me, I was going to let Shaylee decide how we killed him.

chapter eighteen

Gram waited for us at the bottom of the stairs, outside the cavern entrance. She'd bundled herself up in a rainbow wool coat, a pair of white tennis shoes with florescent pink laces tapping impatiently as she waited, white hair floating around her like a living halo.

"About time," she grunted before she hugged me, lips pressing a wet smack against my cheek before fixing Venner with a baleful stare. One of her very sharp nails pointed at him, scrawny index finger jabbing the air in his direction. "One false move," she said before bringing her hands together with a loud crack. She cackled, doing a little jig in place before scowling at him again. "Bug guts. Got me, fairy?"

Venner's usually charming smile slipped from his lips. "No need to be threatening, Lady Rionach," he said. Who? Oh, right. Gram had a Sidhe soul, too. Jeeze, no one ever told me anything. "Your human aspect seems to have affected your bearing."

I took it as an insult, but it just made Gram cackle all over again. "My human form," she said, "has all kinds of secrets. Now, move it, Venemeth."

I waited for Galleytrot to drop the solid barrier he'd erected around the entry to the cavern before parting the shielding. Gram didn't wait, leading the way through, Galleytrot at her heels with Venner jerked along behind by the tether the big dog created. I had to cover my mouth with my hand to keep from laughing at a time when things were no laughing matter. But Gram's attitude helped ease the terrible tension holding me as tightly as the bindings wrapped around Venner.

I forced myself to keep my eyes forward, feeling Quaid and Charlotte close behind me. No looking right into Liam's room with the giant tree hovering over the neatly made bed. And no pausing to peer at the rows of books behind his desk in the archive on the left. I focused on the Gate and what I was going to say to Thalion to convince him to talk to the Queen so I wouldn't have to cross to the Sidhe realm.

Pessimism was winning that particular mental conversation.

Gram stopped, hands on hips, looking up at the old wooden Gate before turning to meet my eyes with her faded blue ones. "Don't ever trust any of them," she said.

"No matter what they say. Ever."

I nodded as I joined her. "I figured out that much on my own." Shaylee sighed as she released the doorstop around the Gate, the vibration of its magic trilling its own song at the loss of her touch.

Gram snorted and took my hand, squeezing my fingers. "You ain't seen nothing, yet, girl." She gestured, green fire dancing over her hand as she touched the Gate with her power. Her Sidhe power. The Gate surged to life, its normal, soft hum that always took me a few minutes to get used to before I could ignore it growing to a song, the voice of the Sidhe realm transferred through wood and metal.

I added my power to Gram's, feeling Shaylee reach out with some reluctance toward the vibrating Gate.

I'm sorry to do this to you, I sent to the princess.

It must be done, she answered. *It's only that I've been away so long and as much as I adore you, the pull of home beckons.*

Wow. I'd totally misread her. *You never mentioned that before.*

The last time we stood here, I feared for our lives, she answered. *And Thalion's call infuriated me. But this time... Sydlynn, if we cross, my heart will ache to remain.*

Fair enough. *You know, no matter what happens, you're not a prisoner.* Unlike Liam, I knew I could survive without her. I had other parts to sustain me, after all. As much as it would hurt, and make my becoming a maji harder, she had to stay by choice.

We are one, now, she sent. *I only warn you so you can steel your heart against the pain.*

Okay then. I felt my demon and my vampire both hug her, the family magic coiling around Shaylee in support. Of all of my alter egos, Shaylee was the most sensitive and, at times, the weakest. But that didn't mean I wanted her to leave.

Not by a long shot.

This might be a moot point anyway, I sent to them all as the Gate's sound built to a crescendo of music, a line of green light glowing around the edges. *If Thalion will talk to the Queen and pursue Ameline, we won't have to cross.*

Such a liar. Like I'd let anyone but me track her down.

Shaylee sighed, but didn't answer.

The Gate sighed as it opened, first a crack, then creaking forward, yawning wide as it fell back toward me, forcing a quick retreat of a few feet. I squared myself as the green power dimmed, only a soft, sparkling rim remaining around the edge of the doorway. Beyond lay green grass, a narrow stone path leading into the distance and rolling hills. The sky seemed dark, no sun in view, no moon either, a kind of perpetual cloudiness dimming the world on the other side.

This felt weird. The ways between the planes were supposed to be off-limits. Even Gatekeepers didn't have regular contact with the Sidhe on the other side. From what Liam told me in his research, this Gate hadn't seen any activity since it was built by his great-great-great grandfather, Connell, aside from the yearly knock to test the keeper's vigilance.

"Time to see if the princeling will come when he's called." Gram poked my ribs with her sharp index finger.

Right. I reached for the veil at the Gate, letting Shaylee's power touch the thin web keeping the Sidhe realm from contacting ours. Her magic stroked the delicate surface, sending ripples like a stone thrown into glassy water out across the barrier, distorting the view.

Thalion, prince, Shaylee's voice joined her touch, echoing in my head. *Come to me.*

I felt his answer, his surprise as he reached back, his cool but eager power pressing to Shaylee's through the veil.

My princess, he sent. *I come.*

Will this take long? Shaylee didn't answer my question. I turned to Gram to ask her, only to see her mouth turn down, eyes locked on the open Gateway. My own gaze was pulled back at the sight of Thalion, mounted on a pure white horse, galloping over the furthest hillock and racing toward us, his long hair and the mane and tail of his huge steed flying.

Like some bad romance novel. I shook my head, breaking free from Shaylee's romantic nature long enough to roll my eyes.

It was going to be one of those days.

Thalion's horse stopped, seeming of its own accord, barely prancing to a halt before the prince slid in a flowing motion to the grass, striding with liquid grace the last few steps to the barrier between planes. Unlike Venner, Thalion's shining silver hair hung unfettered, flowing around him like a cloak, his brilliant green eyes locked on me as he raised one thin-fingered and delicate hand in welcome.

"Your Highness." His voice, cool and precise, actually vibrated with emotion as he fell to one knee and bowed his head. When he looked up, his porcelain skin gleaming in the odd light of his world, two crystal pinpoints of moisture stood in the corners of his wide eyes.

"Prince Thalion." I gently pushed Shaylee aside as I addressed him. "Nice to see you again." Pretty kind of me, considering he'd almost tricked me into crossing over with him the last time I'd seen him when the Gate's knock wasn't answered. Sneaky Sidhe, he had me convinced if I didn't, the barrier would fall and the Sidhe realm would once again be open to ours, making this world vulnerable to the return of their magic and the pending apocalypse that such a return meant. If it hadn't been for Liam's grandfather, Fergus, volunteering to cross, I would probably be in the Sidhe realm already, trapped there because of Thalion's lie.

Thalion's calm expression didn't falter. "And you, my

princess," he said. "Well met." His eyes drifted over the people around me before settling back again. "This is no pleasure calling, Shaylee."

"Sydlynn," I said. "And no."

Shaylee sighed, shaking her head. *He will never admit you exist beyond me*, she sent.

That so? He was about to have a rude awakening.

Honey and vinegar, Gram snapped. *Let the princess handle him. Or do you want to put all of us in danger?*

Grumble, mumble.

Shaylee hugged me gently before rising to take over. I felt her power surge through me, the world tinted green a moment before she bowed our head to Thalion.

"Forgive the urgency of our summoning," she said. "But we have grave news for my mother."

Thalion reached out one hand, pressing it to the barrier. "I am your servant," he said.

Shaylee quickly filled him in on what happened. Thalion's lack of reaction to Venner's presence or the mention a witch carrying stolen Sidhe power was in his playpen kind of pissed me off, but Shaylee held the peace.

When she finished, Thalion's hand dropped as he slowly nodded. "I must admit, there have been unsettling stirrings in the magic of our home." The horse behind him nickered, tossing his big head, one front hoof pawing the ground as if to agree.

"You will speak to mother then?" Shaylee's relief was

strong enough I knew any worry she wanted to leave me was baseless. Again, she hugged me, as Thalion answered.

"I will not," he said. "It is not my message to deliver." Sneaky bastard. Shaylee softly shushed me.

"Not even for me?" She reached out herself, stroking the barrier with her fingertips. A look of ravenous hunger crossed Thalion's face, only a flash, but enough I knew Shaylee completely misjudged him and sealed our fate.

Thalion stepped aside and gestured for us to enter. "Your mother will be delighted to see you," he said.

CHAPTER NINETEEN

I turned to Gram, still holding her hand while Shaylee retreated with a soft apology. "Looks like this is it." Damn, I'd hoped it wouldn't come to this.

Moment of truth—who was I kidding? No way was I backing down, not considering what Ameline had almost accomplished on Demonicon. And, in all honesty, I already admitted to myself Ameline was my responsibility. No matter what Thalion had decided, I knew I'd be crossing over anyway.

How could I trust anyone else to deal with Ameline?

Sucker for punishment or craving danger? I'd leave that for history to decide.

Gram let go of my hand to shed the rainbow jacket, revealing jeans and a t-shirt underneath. I stared. I'd never seen her wear anything but faded dressing gowns and long skirts, fuzzy socks and oversized cardigans. Her thin body looked taller, more filled out. Less granny, more Ethpeal.

I grinned at her and offered her my fist, which she bumped with a wink.

"Let's get this over with," she growled.

I turned to the others, letting Shaylee's magic touch them all, though I left Venner out on purpose.

"Stay close," I said as I shared a bit of her magic with them. "Don't wander."

Quaid just nodded while Charlotte softly chuffed agreement. Galleytrot didn't comment, eyes flashing red fire. I ignored Venner as I turned, drew a breath and stepped toward the Gate.

There's a chance we will never leave, Shaylee sent.

Like I needed to be reminded just as my right foot touched the barrier. Thalion's hand reached toward me, offering assistance, but I avoided his touch, sliding sideways as I parted the veil and crossed over.

I was used to the feeling of riding the veil between Demonicon and home, the rubbery membrane sliding over me. This was an entirely different experience. More like walking through the edge of a giant soap bubble. I worked my jaw as my ears popped, throat tight an instant before my body shifted from one plane to the next. One of my feet suddenly tangled in dense fabric, tripping me, sending me forward, forcing me to take Thalion's hand after all.

A look down at my former casual attire showed me the illusions of the Sidhe realm had taken hold already. I stood there in a flowing white gown trimmed in green and gold, my long, blonde hair hanging over my shoulder, threaded through with sparkling wire and delicate blossoms. The scent of some unbelievably delicious flower flooded my senses, Shaylee's delight bringing my lips up into a smile.

Until I met Thalion's welcoming gaze. Yup, shut her down, and fast.

My fingers explored the pointed tips of my ears, the smooth, cool skin of my arms and face. My neck was longer, too, a choker of woven gold wire hugging the flesh. A pointed metal tiara sat in my hair, poking my printless fingertips.

I felt lighter, as if I could float instead of walk and knew everything physically me was transformed thanks to Shaylee's presence. My demon grumbled her unhappiness at our seemingly weaker body, delicate and fragile, but my vampire didn't say anything, typical of her. At least I had them both with me still, as well as the family magic, though it sat coiled in the bottom of my heart, a sulking child not welcome to come out to play.

Shaylee's mental touch showed me an image of us, though I was familiar with what she looked like. *This is Mother's doing*, she sent. *Her realm, her magic. But if we want her to cooperate, we must go along with her games.*

I was used to games. Still hated them. But surely Queen Aoilainn couldn't be as ridiculous as the two vampire matrons I'd had to wrangle.

Could she?

Sigh.

I turned to look back through the Gate, saw the doorway slowly closing. I panicked, only to have Shaylee soothe me.

We can't leave it open, she sent. *With Venemeth with us, at least there is no risk of someone stumbling on the chamber. But if we leave the Gate open, there are those who might try to cross without our knowledge.*

The Unseelie. I didn't have to ask. *You're sure we can open it again?* Ridiculous worry, really. We were here now and we either would or we wouldn't.

I'm sure, she sent. *You are still anchored to the other side, thanks to the family magic. We will be fine.*

As long as the Seelie Queen didn't find a way to keep us here.

I wished I shared Shaylee's sudden optimism.

I said we could open it again, she sent. *I didn't say anything about being able to cross back.*

Nice of her to clarify and add to my ulcer.

As I turned to tell Thalion it was time to go, I leaped back a step, one hand over my heart. A giant wolf, as big as Galleytrot, stood trembling beside me, long, golden fur standing on end, eyes shining with yellow light. It took me a moment to understand, to reach out and run my hand over the wolf's forehead, stroke her ear.

"Charlotte," I breathed her name. "Wow."

She shook her big head, her shoulder as tall as my hip, a sharp whine emerging from her jaws. She snapped her teeth shut, snorting into the dust before settling on her haunches with her muzzle under my hand.

"This has to be hard for you," I whispered in her perked ear. "Thank you." My eyes drifted over her and to Galleytrot. Who was still himself, if a little beefier, more shaggy. A shadow seemed to hover around him, a dark mist rippling as he moved.

"The shadow of the Wild," he rumbled while the grass around him shifted as though from a stiff breeze. The trail of black led to Venner, also himself, dressed as Thalion was in tight breeches and a long tunic trimmed in gold. He smiled at me, a real smile, but I wished I could smack it from his face.

This wasn't supposed to be fun.

Quaid drew a gasp from my lips and an almost giggle. He creaked as he moved, tall, broad-shouldered body sheathed in metal. But this was no full plate armor like I'd seen in movies, a flowing, liquid armor that fit him perfectly, moving easily as he did, the helmet topped by a flowing white plume, a shield strapped to his left arm and a sword on his hip.

"I feel like an idiot," he growled.

I resisted the urge Shaylee had to blow him a kiss. What was wrong with her?

"Are you going to stand around all day," a woman's voice asked, "or are we going to move on already?"

She stood on my left, on the other side of Thalion, a tall, thin Fey with spiraling dark hair. Blue eyes. Pointed ears. Perfect skin. But I knew her face, had looked at that face almost every day in the mirror.

My face, Sidhized.

I had to try a few times before I finally managed to speak. "Gram?"

She snorted, smoothing her hands over the deep blue gown she wore, her own hair twisted into ringlets full of tiny silver flowers. "It'll do," she said. And winked.

"I don't understand." I glanced at Thalion and then back to Gram. "You look like... me? You?" Did we really look that much alike? It made sense. I looked like Mom. Where did I think my mother got her looks from? But it was uncanny, really.

"Lady Rionach isn't my equal," Gram shrugged, a delicate roll of her shoulders. "So I look like me. Or how I used to appear, I suppose." She frowned, long, thin brows pulling together. "I still don't understand the full gist, but it happened this way last time, too."

"So, because Shaylee is my equal..."

My Sidhe princess finished it for me. *Yes*, she sent. *And, because Mother wishes it so, we look like me here.*

Okay then. I found myself grinning at Gram who grinned right back.

Seeing her like this almost made the whole mess worth it.

"Your Highness," Thalion interrupted with his soft voice. "My Lady." He bowed to both of us. "Companions." I was surprised to find he addressed the others, too. Maybe there was something to this jumping through hoops thing. "If you would follow me. Her Majesty awaits."

chapcer cwency

Thalion sent his horse on alone with a soft whisper and a pat to its neck. "Dubhlainn will alert Her Majesty we are on foot."

I suppressed a grumble at having to walk, only because Shaylee seemed to think grumbling would be rude. If I was going to have to watch everything I said and did because she didn't want to hurt anyone's feelings, this whole trip was going to be a colossal waste of time.

It triggered an understanding in me, though, as we strode along the stone path, Thalion beside me, his hand brushing mine from time to time. On purpose, I was sure. Every time I'd come in contact with the people of one of my egos, I'd always felt connected to them, as if I fit in without effort. I'd always chalked it up to being in danger or running for my life, the fact it took little for me to adjust. I was so used to conflict, I fell easily into the role.

But with Shaylee, I realized that wasn't the case. When I traveled to Demonicon, I remembered feeling angrier, more aggressive. And when I'd faced down the vampire Queens, there had been a powerful attraction to Sebastian, the impulse to stand my ground, a bloodthirstiness to my nature.

Shaylee made me want to sink to the grass and sigh as I listened to Thalion compose bad poetry.

I was seriously going to have to shake her.

At least I finally realized what was happening to me. And it made total sense. Next time I found myself in a position like this one, I had to be more assertive. Case in point. Thalion's hip softly bumped mine, drawing a smile from Shaylee, despite her loyalty to Gwynn.

With a firm frown and a deliberate side step, I put Charlotte between me and the amorous prince. Shaylee didn't complain, but seemed embarrassed while my demon chuckled and my vampire just sighed.

Time to get a grip. Mommy Fey was used to dealing with her soft and kindly daughter. Wait until she got a load of me.

Though the hills looked distant, it seemed like we'd barely walked a quarter mile before we crested them, looking down over a narrow valley with a winding, shining river below cutting a massive forest in two. The deep, rich tones of greens and browns making up the trees morphed as they swayed in the breeze. Pale blue sky, still covered in cloud, hung over the vale. I shivered as Shaylee whispered, *Home.*

"Where is the sun?" I turned to Thalion.

"We left it behind," he said. "When our people came here."

Weird. A whip of wind wound its way over the grass, sending more shivers up my spine and raising goosebumps. I looked to the right, scanning the low bank of heavy, black clouds hunkered close to the horizon, catching the odd flash of lightning, though it was too distant for the thunderclaps to reach us.

"Storm coming," I said, hugging my—Shaylee's—body.

Thalion's gaze lifted as I looked back, his own green eyes locking on the cloud front, a narrow frown on his flawless face. "So it would seem."

Sydlynn, Shaylee sent, a spike of fear in our heart. *The sky is wrong.*

Gram's voice cut in. *Tell me about it.*

What, they never get rain? I started walking again, eyes locked on the storm.

Of course, Shaylee sent. *But by the will of the Queen. Such an event can only bode ill.*

Unless this is her idea? I hated to think badly of Shaylee's mother, but she didn't have the best reputation.

Possible. Shaylee fell silent a moment. *But unlikely. This must be Ameline's doing.*

An unbalance in the magic of the Sidhe. Gram's blue eyes didn't blink. So freaky, still, seeing her look like me. *Could be Ameline. Or something worse.*

What was worse than Ameline?

Hopefully Aoilainn will listen to reason, I sent to them. *She'll have to know something's wrong.*

Shaylee's optimism seemed to stop with her mother. *We can hope*, she sent.

Great.

I followed Thalion, now a stride ahead of me, one of my hands resting in Charlotte's fur as we descended into the valley. Massive oak and maple trees beckoned, the sparkling waters of the river singing as they tripped over polished white stones in the riverbed. A deep inhale filled me with the sweet scent of earth, reminding me so much of Liam I almost wept.

Shaylee was going to ruin me.

Incredibly green grass and a carpet of multi-hued flowers lined the path as we turned in a slow bend to the right, heading for the river. A tall, elaborately curved bridge, spiraling white and gold metal with a base of polished stone, connected the two banks. I half expected a herd of unicorns to trot by and snorted at the idea.

Then again, I'd met dragons, hadn't I? Best not to laugh when I didn't know what to expect.

Anxiety gripped my stomach as I set foot on the bridge, tears rising while my throat tightened. I jerked to a halt, closing my eyes, diving inside to hug Shaylee as my demon and vampire, family magic swirling, joined me.

Listen, I sent. *I can't do this if you're going to be a wreck every five minutes.*

I know. She wrung her mental hands. *I'm sorry, all of you. Forgive me.*

Nothing to forgive. The last thing I needed was her crying for feeling guilty while she cried about coming home. *I realize this has to be hard for you. But we have a job to do, Shaylee.*

We do. She snuffled in my head. *I can do this, Sydlynn.*

I promise, I sent, *when this is over, we'll find a way to come back and spend some time when there isn't a disaster waiting to happen.* Was only fair, after all. My demon was able to go home to Demonicon, though she was born on my plane.

Shaylee seemed to perk at that. *Yes*, she sent, *that would be lovely.* One last sniffle and she settled. *I'll be fine. I promise.*

I opened my eyes to find everyone staring at me, including Thalion, who stood in the middle of the bridge, a quiet but thoughtful look on his face.

"Sorry," I said, "just needed to chat."

"All sorted?" Gram reached for my hand.

"Ready when you are." I just hoped Shaylee could be good to her word and hold it together.

I had a feeling I was going to need all the help I could get.

161

We crossed the bridge without incident, the gushing waters dancing happily beneath our feet. When I touched down on the other side, I looked up at the climbing arch, much like the design of the bridge, just visible inside the tree line.

The entry began to glow as I approached, flocks of tweeting birds flittering around me, a rush of butterflies in purples and golds swooping to settle on my shoulders and my hair. Thalion smiled at me, still cool but with a hint of the feelings he had for Shaylee showing through as he paused on the white stone walk and motioned toward the glowing archway leading deeper into the trees.

"Your Highness," he said, "your realm welcomes you home at last."

CHAPTER TWENTY ONE

I stepped inside the forest, the cool air embracing me, even more earthy and full of delicious scents than the meadow, as the birds settled on branches above, butterflies scattering. I'd thought the path in the trees dark at first, until white globes of glowing light slowly appeared, growing in brightness as I followed the trail, leading the others this time.

I knew this path, the walk to home, recognized each ageless tree, smiled at the antics of the excited songbirds and the curious peekings of rabbits and the occasional doe and her fawn. This was home, the most I'd ever felt at home anywhere, the air itself, the ground beneath my feet, the very trees calling my name, singing their joy at my return.

Heady stuff. I could understand why Shaylee missed it, loved it so. Being embraced by nature itself had a loving quality mere people could never mimic. It was as though the very plane's heart adored me and wanted me to be happy. I'd felt this level of joy in the core of the Node back on Demonicon, but this was entirely different.

Addictive.

I shook free of it while Shaylee fought me, only keeping from shouting at her thanks to my vampire.

Gently, my undead ego sent.

Just keep an eye on me, would you? I shuddered as I realized just how easy it would be to get lost. *You and my demon will have to make sure she doesn't lose it.*

I'm sorry, I'm sorry. Shaylee was weeping again. Really?

Perhaps a change in attitude, my vampire sent. *Some traditional Sydlynn attitude.*

Damned straight. Now she was talking. I purposely tapped into my demon with a smirk.

Shaylee's way is going to get us into trouble, I sent to her as she purred and writhed, amber magic heating the Sidhe's coldness and driving it away. *Feel like making our own brand of badness?*

She roared her approval before shoving her Fey sister aside and hitting me with a blast of demon power.

Syd. Gram's mind met mine. I now felt the chill of her Sidhe side, though I knew Gram well enough she remained in control. *What are you doing?*

I can't rely on Shaylee right now, I sent. *So I'm going to go bulldog and see what happens.*

Gram grunted in my head, but didn't argue. *Just don't blow anything up*, she sent. Laughed. *Without warning me first. Because I want in.*

I loved my grandmother so much.

No time for pleasantries. With Shaylee safely compartmentalized, I put on speed, stalking my way through the forest while Charlotte chuffed beside me. Quaid's mind tried to catch mine, but I shoved him away, knowing from the concern echoing from him he would just give me a hard time.

Too late to stop me, anyway.

I stomped over white stones, past glowing light orbs, scared off the birds and shooed the butterflies. Maybe Queen Aoilainn had a longer memory lane in mind while I allowed my Sidhe side control. She must have known something changed because it took mere moments for the path before me to shift from happy welcome to dark and foreboding before I clomped my way over a footbridge crossing a rushing stream and into a wide clearing surrounded by towering trees.

Spires vaulted above the forest in the background, shining buildings with flashing windows of stained glass, the palace of the Seelie Court reaching for the sky in spun white and gold. I ignored the beauty of it, forcing myself to focus on the close-cut lawn of green before me. And the gathered Sidhe who waited.

I didn't bother with the lines of Fey men and women

in their flowing robes and elegant jewelry, hair cascading around their slender bodies. Or the white columns of twisted marble, draped with flowing white gauze hanging between them. Garlands of flowers in every color possible, more birds, more butterflies. Or the sparkling golden stones leading from the path across the lawn to the small pavilion of more white fabric, as thin and delicate as a dandelion's fluff.

I only had eyes for the tall, blonde woman on the carved, white throne, her green eyes gleaming, face a cold mask as frozen as her seat, white dress a match to mine clinging to her willowy form. I ignored the lovely Fey woman in the deep green gown standing beside the throne in favor of studying Queen Aoilainn. Her long-fingered hands dangled over the arms of her throne as she sat, back straight, crown gleaming on the silk of her hair, waiting for me to come to her.

Mother, Shaylee whispered.

Got that much.

The pressure of her magic was subtle, but insidious, and Shaylee wasn't immune. I guess I wasn't either. Good thing my demon and vampire were unimpressed.

It was their strength keeping me level as I came to a halt at the base of the Queen's throne, my eyes flickering once to the matching one beside her, home to an equally perfect blonde Fey.

Father, my Sidhe princess prompted with a sigh.

Prince Padraic, Gram sent.

He didn't matter. Only the Queen.

She raised one hand, a slow and deliberate gesture, languid. "Welcome home, my daughter," she said in a voice like a long-forgotten melody. "Our court is joyful to greet you, Shaylee."

Yeah, nipping that crap in the bud. "My name is Sydlynn Hayle," I said to the soft gasps of the gathered court. Part of me smirked. I seemed to have that effect on a lot of ruling classes.

The only Fey who didn't respond negatively was the green-gowned woman beside the Queen who flashed a tiny smile, which she covered with her hand.

A possible ally? And with the queen's ear, it looked like.

Aoilainn didn't argue the correction. She just chose to ignore it. "All hail Her Royal Highness, Princess Shaylee of the Seelie." Aoilainn swept to her feet, descending her two steps to take my hands and kiss me coldly on both cheeks. *You are my daughter*, she sent, so powerfully my knees almost buckled. *And I am truly happy to have you home.*

You might change your mind about that, I sent, pushing back with all the power I had at my disposal. Her eyes widened a fraction. I knew no one else saw it. I only caught it because she was so close to me. *When you hear what I have to tell you.*

Never. She stepped back, still holding my hand, her

magic sliding around me, looking for a way in. This wasn't the first time I ended up supremely grateful I'd spent years building my personal shields. No way was I letting her inside. Not with Shaylee all blubbery like she was. I could hear her in the background, begging me to be kind to her mother.

Whatever. Shaylee was clearly delusional. The coldness behind Aoilainn's eyes matched the chill of her skin, heart deep, I had no doubt.

The queen immediately switched tactics, dropping my hand to turn to Thalion.

"You've brought us a great prize," she said. Fixed her gaze on Venner. "And an even greater foe. Well done, my prince."

Thalion bowed while I scowled. "Venemeth is with me," I said. "I'm only here to warn you about an intruder. And then I'm leaving." To hunt down Ameline. I was beginning to think I should have just done that in the first place and the queen be damned.

Aoilainn's perfect brows twitched. "So quickly?" She clapped her hands, the gathering immediately springing to life. "We have as yet to feast."

Like I had time to eat. "This is important," I snapped. "In case you hadn't noticed, Your Majesty," I ground out the honorific, "there's a storm coming."

Sidhe magic didn't fool around. A table appeared as if from nowhere, food flashing into existence to settle on

168

the white surface. A host of chairs with high backs and deep cushions lined the length of the great slab while the court stepped forward once again to slide into their seats. Only the green-gowned Fey waited, hovering by the queen's chair at the end of the table, her pale emerald eyes locked on me.

"Indeed," Aoilainn said. "You will tell me all of it. While we feast."

What was it with monarchs and food? Seriously. The first feast to which I'd been invited wound up with a battle for my demon magic and me and my little sister, Meira, trapped on Demonicon. The second? I almost died, drained by a vampire Queen now resting as a husk of empty in my basement.

This one better have a happier ending.

I sat rather ungraciously across from Quaid. He met my eyes with a warning in his, but didn't comment, not even trying to reach for me anymore. Learned his lesson, I could only guess. Gram took the seat next to me before anyone else could take it. Namely, Thalion. He instead circled around as the queen assumed her place on my right at the head of the table. Quaid was probably less than thrilled to have the Seelie prince beside him, but I felt happier having Gram with me. A glance over my shoulder showed me Galleytrot and Charlotte sitting on their haunches not far away. Four Fey guards stood over Venner, sprawled in the grass.

She won't listen to you, the Unseelie lordling sent. *Watch yourself.*

Like I needed his warning. All of my witchy senses were on high alert, thanks.

Food appeared on my plate as silent servants doled out delicious smelling appetizers, something involving mushrooms and cream. I turned my nose up, leaning in to the queen, noting the green-gowned Sidhe behind her didn't join us to eat.

Bronagh, Shaylee sent. *My mother's first adviser. And a dear friend.*

I still doubted Shaylee's judgment when it came to her own people, but Bronagh seemed welcoming enough, unlike the other Sidhe who stared with blank, cold faces. *Will she help us?* I met Bronagh's bright eyes, found my lips curving to smile in answer to hers.

Possibly, Shaylee sent. *If she believes the queen is in danger, she will do anything to convince Mother to act in her own best interest.*

Then I'd better fill the queen in, hadn't I? But the moment I tried to speak, Aoilainn gestured at my plate.

"Eat first, my dear," she said. "Then we talk."

Gram sampled the food without hesitation, so I shrugged. I seemed to recall stories about normals being trapped by Sidhe food, bound to the realm if they sampled from a Fey plate. But clearly, that wasn't the case for me. I relented and took a bite.

Holy. I thought Demoniconian dishes were delish. This was like something came alive in my mouth and tap-danced across my taste buds. I cleared the delectable serving quickly, trying to formulate what to tell the queen to convince her Ameline was a real threat.

Course after course arrived, my stomach happier than it had been in a long time as Shaylee sighed and welcomed each bite. I let her out a little, knowing she would appreciate this more than the rest of us, feeling her settle and calm.

Speaking of calm, I felt amazing. Things weren't nearly as bad as I thought they were. Ameline wasn't going anywhere. And she'd keep until the feast was over. I glanced at my mother and smiled.

Sorry. Queen Aoilainn.

She smiled back as she touched my hand.

"All of your favorites, my dear." Her green eyes glowed with love for me and I embraced that love, sharing mine with her. Our power mingled gently. "Oh, how I have missed you so, my daughter."

A mouthful of something sharp and tart lit up my mouth and made me moan in delight. Someone brushed my left arm, but when I glanced to the side, we were alone. No matter. I must have imagined it.

But wait. Alone? That wasn't right—

Mother's magic embraces me fully, drawing me

toward her as she leans close and presses her lips to my forehead. My eyes met Bronagh's, see her watching with a nervous expression on her face, as though something is wrong and she doesn't know how to fix it.

Say you'll stay with us forever. Mother's green eyes pull me in, showing me all the incredible things I've forgotten I love about my people, my realm. I sigh and rest my cheek against her shoulder, totally content.

"Mother," I whisper. "I'm so happy to be home."

She laughs, leans back. "But, my daughter," she says as the song of the Sidhe tickles my mind. "You've been here all along."

So I have! How silly of me.

And nothing will ever make me leave.

chapter twenty two

I sit in the open window of my room, looking out over the garden, smiling at the happy trill of the birds. I sigh and lean out to look down over the treetops to the valley.

My heart is happy, and full. But there are moments I cannot bring myself to understand the unrest tickling my senses. My attempts to find Gwynn have left me confused and with an uncharacteristic anger rising in my soul. No one will tell me where he has gone.

Pensive, irritable even, I pluck at the front of my silken gown and wonder where my love has gone. Why has he forsaken me? It's only when my door swings open and sweet Thalion enters, I find myself smiling again.

"Come, my very dear," he says, hands clasping mine, drawing me out of my chambers and into the arching hallway on the other side, "the day is far too beautiful to waste."

Every day is beautiful here. But he is right. No more moping. It's just not like me.

I toss my hair over my shoulder as we run past the wall of mirrors, laughing at how delightful we look together. Thalion's happiness reaches me through our touch, his love a deep and thrumming pulse I sense easily and embrace.

Not fully. Not yet. I still pine for Gwynn. But there will come a time, I'm sure of it, Thalion will take his place. And I am happy for the distraction now.

He leads me down the spiral stairs, across the narrow thread bridge and to the ground, my feet light on the welcoming grass as we run toward the stable and our waiting horses. Thalion pulls me up before him instead, galloping off while I clasp my arms around his neck, breathing his scent of spring and morning glories. His pale cheek feels soft against mine and my heart swells open.

Perhaps he is the one for me after all. Mother will be so pleased to hear it.

His stallion, Dubhlainn spins to a halt, soft mane brushing my arm. Near the point of the river, a blanket has been spread. Small Fey flitter about, their pristine white clothing sparkling as they deposit a delightful array of foods about, scattering as Thalion leaps from the horse and hands me down into his arms.

I sit beside him, tucked against his side as my prince—yes, he is my prince and always will be, I've decided—hand-feeds me morsels while I sigh and listen to the soft sound of his singing.

How could my life be more wonderful?

Something twinges inside me, a feeling of discomfort. I push it down, absorbed in the beauty of Thalion's eyes. When his lips descend to mine, I meet them with my own, breathing his breath as his kiss devours me.

I am so happy.

Aren't I? Shouldn't I be? I pull away from Thalion, sitting up, the stirring in my chest refusing to leave me be. Where once this lovely picnic made me smile, I now see only a mess. The day, bright and cheerful, feels dull to me, the air cold. Even the grass beneath me has a sharp edge to it I abhor suddenly.

"My love." Thalion reaches for me. "What ails?"

I cannot allow him to touch me, cannot abide his gaze either. I spring to my feet, turning and taking Dubhlainn's stirrup, swinging onto the stallion. Thalion calls my name as I push the horse to turn, run away, despite his desire to return to his master.

My magic is stronger than his will. I release him at the base of the bridge and flee for the stairs. My chest feels heavy, as though someone pushes against me, forcing my breaths in panting sobs. I stagger as I trip over the top step, almost falling.

Except she is there to catch me.

"My daughter," Mother's green eyes are calm. Her stillness helps me focus as her power guides and steadies me. "Are you well? I had thought you out with Thalion."

"I was." I weave on my feet, one hand against my forehead, feeling light-headed and fragile. "Mother, I fear there is something not right with me."

She stroked my cheek, her fingers sparking with Sidhe magic, the pressure retreating. "Not at all, my darling," she said with a brief kiss to my cheek. "You need rest, perhaps."

Yes, rest. I follow her as she leads me into my chambers, out onto the low balcony, lying down on a divan, pulling me next to her. With my head cradled on her shoulder, her magic holding me gently, I feel myself finally recovering from the odd malaise.

I wake alone, still on the divan, Mother gone. Feeling much better, I retreat inside to change for supper. But nothing in my selection is suitable. I endure a rush of disgust for everything offered to me by my servants, send them scurrying with angry words and snaps of magic.

Each and every gown I shred with power and send fluttering to the floor. Ugly. All of it, ugly. And a lie.

What lie? I draw a breath against the tightness holding me captive, heart pounding as my gaze rises and I meet a pair of blue eyes in my mirror.

I leap with terror at the sight of the furious young

woman reflected over my shoulder. A human! Here? I spin, fear pounding away at my soul. No human can be here.

But no. The room is empty. I am alone, after all.

Why did she seem so familiar?

Mother is unhappy with me at dinner, Thalion sullen, but I do not care. Refuse to talk. Who was that girl? And from where do I know her? I pick at my food before rising to retreat.

"You haven't finished." Mother reaches for my hand, but I snatch mine away before she can touch me.

"Just leave me alone, won't you?" I run from her, from Thalion as he calls my name, fleeing yet again to my quarters, sending my weeping servants away. I collapse on my bed and sob.

A soft step, a warm hand on my back and Bronagh settles next to me. Her clear green eyes are full of warmth, her touch the same I remember from my childhood. My mother's oldest adviser and my dear friend rubs soft circles between my shoulder blades to soothe me.

"I'm ill," I whisper.

"You're not," she answers. "Sleep. And remember there is more to you than she lets you feel."

Bronagh leaves me alone to ponder her words, to think on the life of illusions Mother has spun for us here.

This is wrong. My home, my life. Everything is the

way it should be and yet, I can't help but know, in my deepest soul, it is all a terrible lie.

Still weeping, I fall into a troubled slumber.

Darkness engulfs me. Glowing amber eyes emerge from the black, curving horns shining in demon fire as the red-skinned creature lunges forward, snarling my name. I flee from her, further into the shadows, only to feel the chill of the grave slide over my skin. I huddle, weeping, as a shining white vampire, her eyes flaring with spirit magic, thunders her fury.

I barely escape her, following the thread of rainbow magic, riding it like a river, desperate to escape. But there is no escape. I see her then, the young woman, the human, her face a mask of rage. Multi-hued magic flashes around her as she rises above me, a giant. The vampire and demon join her, becoming her while the river of power pins me to the ground.

I try to fight back, but she is so strong. And so familiar. Part of me wants to welcome her, but I am afraid.

Until she touches me. And my heart opens again.

"Syd," I whisper.

No longer afraid.

Furious.

chapter twenty three

Shaylee wasn't the only one feeling a tad bit pissed off. I sat up in her bed, my hands shaking, my demon roaring so loudly I had to yell at her to make her stop so I could focus.

Syd. Shaylee's mental voice vibrated with a mix of anger and regret. *Oh, Syd. I'm so sorry.*

Last time you say that, I sent back, trying not to focus my rage on her. *Right?*

Yes. She hissed, essence crackling with earth magic. *She dared to manipulate and coerce me. Her own daughter.* Was she really that naive? Well, not anymore. I'd take angry Shaylee over sad and pining Shaylee any day.

Time to kick some Sidhe queen ass. But as I leaped from the bed, motion near the balcony caught my attention. I pulled my power around me, all of it, reveling at the feeling of being free again, my demon and vampire joining the family magic in pushing the limits just as three figures slid into my room.

I almost cried out at the sight of two of them. Wasn't that Liam? Standing next to me? But it wasn't a mirror, was it, and I was Shaylee here in the realm. But there they were, only a few feet away...

Wait, no. Not Liam. My heart almost leaped from my chest. Liam was Ameline. But before I could lash at him/her with magic, I felt his touch on my mind.

Not my hated enemy at all. The soft mind reaching for mine belonged to Liam's grandfather, Fergus.

And the mirror image of me? Gram. Right. I shivered at the sight of them together, a very private and very vain part of me wondering if Liam and I looked that fantastic as a couple.

Sheesh, Syd. Way to focus on the important things.

The third figure gripped the skirt of her deep green gown and locked gazes with me.

"Syd?" Gram took a step closer, a frown on our face, shifting my attention.

I tossed aside Shaylee's long hair with a grunt of temper. "Yeah," I said. "Present and accounted for."

Gram let out a sigh of relief while Fergus bowed to me with a grin so sweet my heart ached for Liam all over again. "Nice to see you again, Miss Hayle," he said in his grandson's voice.

"Hey, Fergus." It was hard not to run to him and hug

him, just to remind me why I was here. Or part of the reason. I let my eyes settle on Bronagh again before I bobbed a nod to her. "You three here to rescue me or something?"

Gram's grin made her Fey influenced face look much more human. "Something like that," she said. "Leave it to you not to need us."

Shaylee's anger settled as she flinched. "We've straightened things out internally," I said. "But there are a few external matters I still have to deal with."

Gram nodded quickly while Fergus's smile fell to a sad frown.

"Please," he said. "Be cautious."

"Not that I've been asked," Bronagh said in a soft voice of velvet, "but I agree with Fergus. Perhaps if you let me speak to the Queen on your behalf? Shaylee can assure you I only have your best interests in mind."

I believed her. "You're part of the reason I woke up, aren't you?"

Her cheeks flushed. "I offered some encouragement," she said. "I adore my queen, but she isn't thinking clearly. There are times we must think for her."

Okay then. I was going to get along with Bronagh after all.

Fergus reached for my hand, his concern clear on his earnest face. "Now that you've broken free of the queen's coercion, she will stop at nothing to keep you here. Even if it means imprisoning you."

A spatter of colored sparks fell from my hands as my anger surged. "She can try." It took a moment to pull myself back under control. "I couldn't care less about what she wants," I said. "Or changing her mind for that matter." Bronagh nodded sadly. "More importantly, how much time have we lost?"

Fergus shrugged. "What you think of as time moves differently here," he said. "Perhaps a few hours have passed on the other side of the Gate."

That made me feel a little better. Until I tensed, remembering I hadn't come here alone. "Where's Charlotte?" Nice of me to think of the weregirl finally.

"I can lead you to her." Bronagh held out her hand. "But we have to move quickly. It won't be long before the queen realizes you've slipped her power."

Hurry was my middle name.

I followed the Fey adviser out onto the balcony and down the half-hidden staircase I'd missed earlier, Gram and Fergus close behind. Of course, Shaylee knew it was there. Hadn't thought it important enough to focus on.

I had a lot to teach her about watching her own back. And hopefully, we had the time for her to learn.

Night only came to the Sidhe realm when the queen thought it necessary, so we found ourselves trying to mingle with the few other Seelie we encountered. Most of them simply bowed to me and Bronagh and didn't ask questions, so we moved along quite quickly. I caught the smell of dogs and kennels moments before Bronagh led us from the white stone path and behind a copse of trees.

My gut twisted at the sight. A patch of bare earth housed a stake, a thick post of seasoned wood. A glittering silver spike pinned a length of shining chain to the stake, ending in a collar around the golden wolf's neck.

That wasn't the worst part, not by a long shot. They'd chained and collared my bodywere. She lay panting on her side, huge rents dug in the ground beneath her, slashing cuts marring her beautiful coat, blood running down her sides to pool in the earth. Charlotte still clawed at the ground, trying to pull herself forward while she choked on the tight collar, coughing as she fought.

Three Sidhe stood around her, all with sparkling golden whips, dripping blood, faces cold and blank.

Not for long.

If they saw me coming, they had barely a moment to register my presence as my power lashed out and drove the three face-first into the ground. A snap of air power wrapped the whips around their necks and pulled tight, choking them in turn, as I stomped my way across the dirt and to Charlotte's side.

Gram's growl of fury and surge of magic took over from me as I focused on the fallen weregirl. Knowing my grandmother would come up with a suitable punishment for the three attackers, I let my magic go, sliding it around Charlotte and into her damaged body.

So much pain. Broken ribs, shattered leg bones, a powdered vertebra. Tears welled in my eyes, not Shaylee's this time, as I threaded through Charlotte's body with spirit magic and began to reverse the damage. My Sidhe princess sobbed in my head, hugging herself while I worked. I let my demon and vampire comfort her, unable to bring myself to forgive Shaylee for allowing this to happen to Charlotte.

Not yet, anyway.

Charlotte's yellow wolf eyes never left mine, her body recovering quickly. I slicked the blood from her coat with a surge of fire magic, helping her rise, feeding her energy until she shook herself, a low growl of fury making her tremble.

I turned to find Gram and Fergus tying up the now-unconscious Sidhe with their own whips, Bronagh standing to one side, eyes averted as though unwilling to be part of the assault. I couldn't blame her when I thought about it. These were her people. And yet, they'd hurt Charlotte thanks to Bronagh's queen.

Messy, my mixed emotions. Very messy.

Gram came forward to hug Charlotte before meeting my gaze.

"They won't wake," she said. "And when they do, it will be to so much pain they'll wish they hadn't."

Worked for me. "Galleytrot?"

Fergus's nervousness told me the big hound was in as much trouble as Charlotte, if not more.

"He is heavily guarded," Bronagh said.

"So?" I let my power flood around me. I'd take them all on if I had to.

The advisor nodded without further argument. "This way."

Not far, it turned out. I could feel the black dog as soon as we rejoined the path and turned off into another clearing. But he felt strange, distant and as I approached the dozen or so Sidhe in the same shining metal armor Quaid wore—one more person to worry about— and I felt my fury build to murderous.

"Where is he?" It was hard to keep a calm face while I shook from rage, but I did a half-decent job. Partly because Shaylee finally stepped up and did her Sidhe thing.

"Your Highness." One of the guards bowed as his eyes flickered to Bronagh. "Advisor."

"Oengus," Shaylee said through me while Bronagh stayed silent. "My lord. Where is the hound?"

He pointed to a small hole in the ground, a black scar in the dirt. "Where your mother sent him, Your Highness," he said.

"Bring him to the surface." I allowed Shaylee her anger, let her deal with them. But only after she whispered, *Please, I must make this right.*

The one she'd named Oengus exchanged a look with another guard. *He's nervous*, she sent to me.

"Now, my lord," she said.

"I can't do that without Her Majesty's order." A spine? How original. Or maybe he was just more afraid of the queen, which made sense.

He was about to find out he was scared of the wrong Sidhe.

Shaylee's magic slammed into his chest without warning, the front plate of his armor crumpling as he went down in a heap. "I said," she leaned us forward and spoke with a light, gentle voice, "bring him up."

I had to hand it to the guards. They didn't give in willingly. But they were no match for a very furious Princess Shaylee, a pissed-off demon, a vampire with a temper, a snarling werewolf with revenge on her mind, two witches and a former Gatekeeper.

Syd's team, twelve. Sidhe, zero.

Hell yeah.

It irritated me Bronagh stood back and let us do all the work, but again, I guessed I understood why. Still. She'd come this far, helped us this much. The least she could do was go all in.

I left Gram and the others to mop up the quick, dirty fight, ignoring the crumpled, shining piles of unconscious guards as I stepped to the lip of the hole. It seemed bottomless, wider at the mouth than I first thought, though it had to be a cramped space for the giant dog.

My stomach fluttered as I looked down into all that emptiness, my fear of heights driving me back a step to take a deep breath. Images of falling from an elevator toward the Parade on Demonicon still haunted me.

But this was for Galleytrot. I had to rescue him.

My vampire gently touched my mind. *We have means*, she sent. *Think of him, remember?*

How had I forgotten? I reached for her, focused on where I wanted to be and went.

The teleportation lasted a moment, the soft flutter of shadow depositing me into darkness so deep I staggered, reaching for support. And came in contact with fur, damp and filthy. Something grunted, the sound of movement sending shivers down my spine as two pinpoints of red light cast a bloody wash over everything.

"Syd." Galleytrot groaned, tried to rise. I held him down, feeling him with my energy. They'd drained him, the bastards. Left him at the bottom of the hole almost powerless.

They'd pay.

She'd pay.

Shaylee had the answer, before I could figure out what to do. *We're surrounded by earth*, she sent. *And though he can't reach it in his condition, it is an infinite source to help him recover.*

I felt it then, when Shaylee allowed me to touch the still bubbling power. The subtle pull still going on, as the very ground around us sucked at Galleytrot's energy. With Shaylee to guide me, I shocked the contact and reversed it, sending a flood of magic back the way it had come.

For the second time since this began, Galleytrot howled his rage, surging to his feet as his magic returned to him. I leaned against him while he absorbed as much as he could, stronger than I'd ever felt him.

"We have to go." I patted his shoulder, now almost on level with mine.

"Syd," he said. "This is twice I've failed you." So much regret and guilt, I could barely stand it.

I hugged him around the neck and breathed in his scent of thunderstorms and spring rain. "You've never failed me," I said. "It's the other way around. I should have kept Liam safe. And I should never have let Aoilainn trick me like that."

"You're going to do something about it, I take it?" Good humor returned to his voice, if only a little.

"Planned on it," I said. "Feel like giving me a hand?"

"Thought you'd never ask." He growled softly, big tongue swiping over my cheek. "Thank you, Syd."

Can we teleport with him? I reached for my vampire only to have her pause.

Possibly, she sent. *But we're a long way down. Perhaps the veil?*

Right. She was full of brilliant ideas. I grasped the edge of the Sidhe veil, feeling my demon grunt even as Shaylee did most of the work. It parted before me, feeling different than what I was used to. That soap bubble touch slid over me as I pulled Galleytrot into the edge and let it carry me back to the surface.

As much as I loved riding the Demonicon veil, the Sidhe one gave me the willies and I was happy to find myself stepping out and onto the grass. Gram and Fergus spun from where they peered down into the hole, Charlotte trotting to my side to head-butt Galleytrot.

"One more," I said, turning to Bronagh who watched from the edge of the clearing. "Quaid."

She nodded while Fergus sighed and met my eyes with a guilty gaze. "He'll be the hardest to retrieve," the advisor said. "But since you plan on confronting the queen anyway, we'll at least have access to him."

She had him. Of course she did.

The bitch.

We'd just see about that.

CHAPTER TWENTY FOUR

This time, I knew I had to make an entrance. If power was all Aoilainn understood, I'd show her just who and what she was dealing with.

No promises the Sidhe realm would still be standing when I was done with her.

As much as I was turned around and lost, Shaylee knew exactly where we were going and, with some help from her magic and mine, shortened the trip by altering the path much as her mother had done on our initial approach. It was only then I understood just how fluid the realm was, how easy it could be to bend and manipulate, to create in exactly the shape I wanted.

Tempting. And therein lay the problem, didn't it? Queen Aoilainn had her own way for so long, controlled everything for centuries, the idea I would rebel against her had to be driving her crazy.

Wicked. The crazier the better.

Bronagh stayed at my side when I entered the court clearing, much to my surprise. The queen waited for me on her stupid throne, the crown prince next to her, the same calm, cold expression on both their faces. And Quaid, still in his armor, standing at attention by her side. I sent a wave of magic out from me, right and left, tumbling Sidhe royals like ten-pins, sending them shrieking in fear, sobbing out their poor little Fey terror as they fled.

No time for histrionics.

Aoilainn didn't move or fight back as I came to a charging halt before her, my posse at my back and a whole crap-ton of magic preceding me, ready to smear her against her pretty white palace. Instead, she merely bowed her head in a slow nod, eyes flickering to Bronagh before returning to me.

"My daughter," she said in her melodic voice, the trailers of her magic trying to siphon away my spirit, calling to Shaylee. "Come to me, my child."

It might have worked the second time. But if I had any doubts as to Shaylee's current loyalties, not to mention her state of mind, they shattered as the Sidhe princess lashed out with her power and slapped her own mother across the face.

Aoilainn's head rocked back, shock finally registering.

One slim hand rose to touch her cheek as my Sidhe ego snarled her fury.

I reached for Quaid while Shaylee snapped at her mother. "How dare you treat me like a slave?" He felt empty. Silent. Too silent. The queen had him thralled. "Your own daughter?" I had to find a way to break him out of it. My magic reached for him, my demon boosting our touch, but he didn't react. "I've only longed for you, Mother, for my return home. And this is how you treat me?" My vampire joined us, but still nothing.

What had she done to him?

"Enough." I pushed Shaylee back to grumble and sulk inside me. "I've about had it up to here," I slashed one hand across the air in front of my nose, "with your absolute idiocy." The Queen flinched, anger showing at last. Good. Let it. "No more screwing around."

Aoilainn's lips twisted at my rude language. "You invade my realm," she said, voice pulsating with emotion, "assault my people and expect me to listen to anything you have to say?"

Of all the conniving... "Your precious realm is in danger, you fool." I wanted to shake her. Seriously. "An intruder with a stolen Sidhe soul is here, right now, doing who knows what. And meanwhile, one of your Gatekeeper's lives hangs in the balance. While you sit around being selfish." I took a step closer. She had to understand. "That means the Gate is unprotected." Was that a bit of concern or indigestion? Who knew with the Seelie Queen. "No Gatekeeper. That means everyone is in danger, your Majesty. Including you and your precious little realm. What if the Unseelie find a way through? Or someone seizes control of the Gate?" I couldn't control my trembling. "This is a huge problem, in case you've missed it. Not tomorrow. Not next week. Right. Now."

Seriously.

"My queen," Bronagh's hands rose, appealing to her ruler. "Please, I beg you to listen."

Aoilainn's power rose, sucking at me as the earth had drawn on Galleytrot. "You will be mine again," she said, leaning toward me, face twisted from beautiful to absolute need.

I would have slapped her myself if Shaylee hadn't done that already. Instead, I pushed Aoilainn away with the combined energy at my disposal. She fell back, panting, perfect hair a little mussed.

She didn't give warning, leaping to her feet, all the pressure of the Seelie court coming to bear on me. For a moment, I wavered, pouring magic into my protections, knowing it wouldn't be enough, not against the ruler of this realm.

Not until the tingle of the maji power rose in answer.

Aoilainn fell back with a cry of fear as creation magic shattered her attack, drawing all the pieces of her broken glamour into itself. The Sidhe queen cut off her power as she sagged into her throne, skin sinking a moment, face crumbling with age before she sucked in a deep breath and recovered her unnatural beauty.

"How?" Aoilainn's green eyes shone with tears.

"There's a war coming," I said, letting her feel the maji inside me. "And unless you help us, there's a good chance we're going to lose." Okay, I didn't know that for sure. But if Ameline became maji first, I had no doubt we'd be in serious trouble.

"It's truth she speaks, my queen," Bronagh said, climbing to stand next to Aoilainn. "Put aside your ancient need and listen to Sydlynn, I beg you. Our people are in danger from a terrible force and unless we are willing to act against them, all will be lost."

She had to be talking about the Brotherhood, not just Ameline. But how did she know about them? Clearly she wasn't one of these weak-minded, glamour-captive Sidhe. My respect for Bronagh went up a few more notches.

Instead of answering my challenge or answering her most trusted advisor, Aoilainn turned away, one hand over her face as she spun sideways in her throne. Bronagh's sad expression as she shook her head and shrugged told me everything I needed to know.

"Fine," I snarled. "Your realm will probably be the first to fall and I personally won't come running when you finally ask for help."

I reached for Quaid, grabbed his hand, pulled him to

me.

Time to go.

Too bad he had other ideas.

chapter twenty five

I had about a split second of warning before Quaid's power slammed up in a wall between us, pushing me back from him even as a whip of green Sidhe magic lashed at my feet. I stumbled away, shock winning for about another heartbeat or so before I understood the nature of his thrall.

"You've given him a Sidhe soul." Of course, she had. Made total sense. And now, thanks to his thrall, while she controlled Quaid's human mind, the fallen Sidhe inside him was free to act. "You go too far."

She flickered her fingers at me, still refusing to turn, or even speak.

Expecting me to hurt my friend. Yeah. Classy.

Gram's mind dove into mine as Quaid pulled the sword from his hip and stalked toward me with soft chiming sounds, his fluid metal armor flowing like a second skin. I had to duck under the swish of the blade and back pedal further while Charlotte and Galleytrot growled. But hesitated.

We have to reach Quaid, Gram sent. *The only way to do that is to have him shed the Sidhe soul.*

Great idea. *How?* I stopped backing off, pulling on my newly risen maji magic, creating a shield of my own. Wrapped it around one arm as a length of glowing light burst from my other hand. Quaid's next swing bounced from my protected left arm, sparks of rainbow magic flying. He was much stronger than me and I knew without the extra maji boost my arm would be, at the very least, numb if not broken.

It was difficult to focus my magic on his mind while swinging my glowing weapon at him in an effort to just keep him off me. Whoever possessed his body was obviously a fighter.

I wasn't.

Sydlynn, Shaylee rose to the surface of my mind. *Let me.*

And me. My demon shouldered her way to Shaylee's side.

Right. I wasn't alone in this, not by a long shot. Though it was so hard to step away from my body, a passenger, feeling myself move but knowing I had no control over what I did.

Whatever happens, I shot off to Charlotte and

Galleytrot, *stay the hell out of it.*

Neither answered but their unhappiness told me I'd better wrap up things quickly if I expected them to hold off.

The moment I released my demon and Shaylee to act, I went from clumsy stumbler, barely holding Quaid off, to fluid warrior.

Cool. Just. Cool.

No time for self-appreciation, my vampire sent. *It's our job to free him.*

Gotcha. *Can you suck the soul out of him?* Rather a disgusting suggestion, in my opinion. My body dropped to the ground in a split-leg crouch, shield arm taking Quaid across the knees as the glowing sword I held rang against the metal protecting both of his ankles.

Sydlynn. My vampire's disappointment sat heavy in my mind. *Really.*

Sorry. I had no idea I could do back flips. And though I looked like Shaylee here, would my human body pay for it when I got home?

No time to worry about it while I landed softly, only to spring forward and strike Quaid across the side of his helmet, sending him staggering back.

My pair of egos were really quite good.

We need to break the thrall, my vampire sent while my demon and Shaylee pushed their advantage, sending Quaid back toward the pavilion and the now-observant

Aoilainn. Nice of her to sit up and take notice at last. *Quaid's mind is much stronger than the Sidhe inhabiting him. Once we return control to him, he can expel the soul himself.*

While I dodged to the left, spinning in a circle with my long, blonde hair flying, narrowly avoiding losing the locks to the edge of Quaid's blade, I focused my mind on his, prodding the green shielding around his consciousness, looking for a way in.

I'd give Aoilainn one thing. She was good. Very good. Centuries of experience with making those around her do whatever she wanted clearly paid off, and not to our benefit.

A bit of despair crept in until my vampire jabbed me out of it.

Focus, she sent. *She is Sidhe only. You are maji, or will be some day. What others create, you can control, Sydlynn Hayle. That is the true power of the maji.*

Anything? Wow, that was a revelation. I mean, I knew I could use the maji power to create, and to siphon power. But control the magic of others?

Holy.

Don't get cocky, Gram sent in a flash. *Listen to your vampire. But pay attention. Like she said, you're not maji yet. But you have access to some of the abilities. Use them and hurry up about it. As much as I'm liking this new shape, I want to go home. I'm missing my soaps.*

Snort. Leave it to Gram to take the edge from

anything.

Focus. Right. Why had I never explored the maji power? I really had to stop being so complacent about the magic I had access to. It seemed like I just sort of fell into routine and a bit of boring normalcy when things were quiet, with no desire to prod any of my magicks for further info. It wasn't until the crap hit the fan I found myself wishing I'd done something about it sooner.

We've all been complacent, my vampire sent. *No longer. There is too much at stake. Now free Quaid and let's find Ameline.*

I slid inside the maji power, feeling the pull of all my magicks as my body twisted and spun and bent at odd angles, fighting Quaid still. I didn't feel an ounce of weariness or even an ache, which made me worry more. But that was for later. In this moment, as I allowed the maji energy to absorb me, fill my core while my other magicks fed into it, the world

Went.

Away.

Not away, precisely. But the glamour did. The shining, sparkling waters were just ordinary. The flowing white fabric nothing to get excited about. The ultra-green grass needed to be watered. The towering palace could use a good scrubbing. Even Aoilainn's perfect face seemed old, the same drawn and thinning appearance I'd caught the edges of when my maji power pushed her back.

Interesting. I could now see the overlay of the Sidhe soul pressing down on Quaid, his magic eyes closed behind it. It was simplicity itself to slide inside the soul, past it, to my friend. To feel his heartbeat, enter his thoughts.

His dreams. Aoilainn had Quaid convinced we were on our way back to the Gate with Ameline in our possession. He felt proud, happy. Couldn't stop staring at the image the queen created of me, the real me only better. Sidhized. I felt his love and the struggle in his heart even as I reached out with my maji power and woke him up.

The soul clinging to him wailed in agony and fled as Quaid's conscious mind jerked awake. Shaylee and my demon stopped fighting instantly as the young Enforcer froze, eyes locked, not on me, but on someone over my shoulder. I turned to see Gram smiling at him.

"Syd." Quaid staggered, dropping the sword. "What's going on?"

"You've been asleep," I said, as his gaze flickered to me and back to Gram. "Nice dreams?"

Quaid shook his head, turned to glare at the queen. "She did this?"

"Don't you worry," I said, facing off with the now-furious Aoilainn. "This isn't over. But it will be very soon."

"Yes." Aoilainn flowed to her feet, arms raised while Bronagh fell back with a quick shake of her head in warning. "But not in your favor, Sydlynn Hayle."

Sidhe troops rushed from the surrounding trees, ranks upon ranks of them, surrounding us in their shining armor and pulsing with magic.

A quick calculation told me I could probably make a hole in them and try to run for it, but I had no idea if the glamour the queen spun would simply send me in circles or not. Probably. So running was out.

I was tired of running, anyway.

"You are ordered to leave my realm," the queen said in her throbbing voice. "Thalion Prince will lead you to the Gate and ensure you depart. But." She stepped down from her throne, green magic sparking around her. "You will leave my daughter here, with me." One hand swept over the empty space beside her.

The ground rumbled, erupted, vines twining from the upturned earth, sprouting into a tall shape quickly formed to a woman's body.

I was about to protest Shaylee wouldn't be able to stay without a form to inhabit.

Looked like the queen thought of that, too.

"You would imprison your daughter in a fake form just to get your way?" I shook from the intensity of Shaylee's rejection as well as my own. "Selfish queen. Time to grow the hell up."

My Sidhe princess sent her own disdain in a rush of rejecting energy.

Aoilainn's beautiful face twisted, lips thinned, eyes wide in fury. "Then none of you will ever leave." She raised her arms above her head, the ground rumbling again. I spun toward my friends, reaching for Gram just as the earth gaped open and swallowed her up. Fergus, Charlotte, Galleytrot, and yes, Quaid, all drawn into the ground that resealed behind them.

My magic dove after them, but they were already gone.

The bitch.

I turned on her with a snarl, maji magic poised. "I can strip the glamour from this place," I said. "Turn your realm into the ordinary, crumbling truth it is. Return them now."

Aoilainn trembled, but refused to relent. "Try," she said.

Can I do it? I reached for my vampire who sighed.

You and your big threats, she sent. *Perhaps if you were full maji. You can possibly affect some things directly, but there is too much magic here for you to destroy all at once.*

Crap. Bluff called. I stared at Aoilainn in frustration, hands clenched but unable to do anything but see past the lies she created around her.

Not much good to me.

"I didn't think so." Aoilainn's gentle tremors stilled as

she smiled, confidence returning as she gracefully retook her seat. "You will give up my daughter's soul," she said, "or I will kill your precious friends one at a time."

She'll kill them anyway, my vampire sent.

Shaylee choked on a sob, but agreed.

No deal. "If you touch one of them," I said, empty threat burning in my throat, "I'll kill you myself."

Aoilainn didn't look all that worried. "You have only a short time to change your attitude. I will have the first body brought to you shortly." She clapped her hands, a lazy motion as though she'd grown bored of our conversation. "Take her away."

A dozen Sidhe soldiers surrounded me. I could have taken them out, easy. But I had to find the others first. Damn it.

Damn it.

Bronagh's green eyes watched as I was taken away and I wondered if I could still count on her to help. At least the queen hadn't seemed angry about her advisor's latest choice in allies. I'd hate to think I was the cause for her suffering after she'd tried to do what was right.

A short walk while I seethed, through sighing trees and down white-stoned paths and I found myself being shoved into a small opening at the base of a tree. The large oak shuddered as its roots formed bars over the doorway, trapping me just below ground with a clear view across from me.

As the silver-booted feet of my guards marched away, I ground my teeth at the sight of Venner smiling and waving from his own prison directly opposite.

chapter twenty six

"I see negotiations with Her Majesty are going well." Venner's chuckle made my temper bubble. I briefly considered something nasty, but shoved it away.

No time for pettiness. Not while I had my friends to save. Not to mention catching Ameline.

I turned my back on Venner, leaning against the clay wall, arms crossed over my chest as I drew some deep breaths to quiet my temper.

Can we find the others? I directed my question at Shaylee.

She didn't feel hopeful. *It's possible I could locate one of them*, she sent.

My demon growled. Yeah, bad idea. No doubt Aoilainn would just strike at someone else while I tried to do a singular rescue. And I was kind of attached to all of them, thanks.

What about my maji magic? I reached for it again, felt it humming softly in my heart.

It allows you to see past illusions, my vampire sent. *So if we were able to locate the others, I'm sure you'd have no trouble rescuing them. But again, you'd be doing so one at a time.*

Mother will be careful, now that she understands how powerful you are. Shaylee hugged me gently. *I'm so sorry, Sydlynn. This is all my fault.*

No, I sent. *It's Ameline's. And Aoilainn's. Shaylee, will Bronagh try to help us again?*

She may, as long as Mother doesn't punish her. My princess shuddered. *She took such a great risk, I hope she's all right.*

Right. Who knew what Aoilainn had planned for the Fey woman now that we were in the bag? *So, options? I need options, y'all.*

There is only one I can see, my vampire sent, ever so softly.

And it was unacceptable. *I'm not giving you up, Shaylee.*

She didn't comment.

Didn't have to.

How much did this suck?

"You know," Venner's voice penetrated my private conversation with myself. "If we could reach my court, it's likely we could convince His Majesty to assist us in finding and stopping Ameline."

Yeah, right. "Nice try, Venner."

He may be right, my vampire sent. *Even I was aware, back when I was created, great animosity existed between the two Sidhe courts. If the King of the Unseelie can see some personal benefit in helping us, we might be able to convince him to assist.*

No, Shaylee sent. *It won't work. They've had the same agreement for centuries. Neither crosses over into each other's territories. On threat of war.*

Just what we needed. Another mess.

Quick footfalls approached, turning me around. A green gown swished before Bronagh crouched to look down into my prison, her emerald eyes shining as she glanced over her shoulder.

"Are you well?" She clutched the roots with both hands. "I worried she might harm you after all."

"We're fine," I said. "Can you find the others?"

Bronagh shook her head, face falling. "I'm sorry," she said. "The queen no longer trusts me."

"Thanks for the help," I said, hopes dashed she might be able to find a way to rescue my friends and grandmother.

"I hate to suggest it," Bronagh said, "but knowing my queen's convictions, unless you want the deaths of those you love on your hands, you might have to do as she asks."

My whole body twitched in rejection. "Absolutely not."

Bronagh sagged to the grass, tears welling in her eyes. "I know what I'm asking of you," she said. "How terrible this is. But Sydlynn, we both also know the threat coming. And the importance of readying our realms for their assault."

"You know about the Brotherhood." Damn it. I hated she was right.

"I do," she said. "Some of us are aware. Are paying attention."

"Then you also know I can't give up Shaylee," I said. "I won't be maji anymore. And my role will change." I refused to say I would be useless. But that was how I felt.

Bronagh chewed her lower lip a moment before nodding quickly. "I have an idea," she said. "But you have to trust me."

Big leap, even for someone who'd helped me already.

She is trustworthy, I swear it, Shaylee sent. *Bronagh has always been my most powerful supporter against Mother.*

"Let's hear it," I ground out while my jaw ached from clenching my teeth.

"You release Her Highness," Bronagh said. "Allow her to inhabit the form Aoilainn has created. Let the queen become happy, complacent. And, when the time is right and she allows Shaylee more and more freedom, I will bring her personally to the Gate and you can be reunited."

Shaylee gasped in my head, spoke through my lips. "She will kill you for such a betrayal."

Bronagh's face darkened. "My queen is not the

person I've served all these centuries," she said. "The Aoilainn I adored would have been the first to demand all Sidhe pay attention to the threat of the sorcerers."

I sank against the dirt, heart pounding, not wanting to even consider this plan, but deep down, knowing it was our best option.

There is only one solution here, Sydlynn. Shaylee's sadness increased as she stretched herself inside me, pushing the boundaries of our connection. *I have to go to Mother. And trust Bronagh's plan will work.*

I didn't care about the whole maji thing, at the moment, though it hovered in the back of my mind. *I'm not losing you.*

It's the only way to save everyone, she sent.

I thought you said she'd probably kill us all anyway? There, that should fix it.

I will personally ensure your safety, she sent. *If Mother betrays you, I will leave the form she's made for me and never reincarnate again.*

Why did she have to sound so logical? And so right?

What about this form she's made you? There had to be a good reason to keep her with me. Desperation tore at my insides while she began to pull away. My demon grasped for her while the family magic pooled deep inside, thrumming with grief. *It can't survive like a real body.*

It's been done before, Shaylee sent. *Though at great personal cost to the soul inhabiting it. Mother is creating a prison for me. I will be forced to use most of my magic just to keep it alive.*

Wow. And I thought my mom was a bitch sometimes.

I can't let you go. My hands shook as I stood there, head down, tears welling in my eyes, ignoring Bronagh who hovered and watched. *Not to that kind of non-life.* I drew a shaking breath. *I love you, Shaylee. And I need you. How can I just let you leave? There has to be something else we can do.*

Shaylee wept even as she pulled even further from us. *It's my decision,* she sent. *And I choose to stay.* She hesitated before stammering, *I'm tired of all the fighting, Sydlynn. I'm just not strong enough. You see that, don't you?* She shook inside me, a trembling, fragile leaf on a brisk wind. *I've been nothing but a hindrance to you since I woke. Doing what Mother wants will free me from all that is to come while allowing you to escape.*

You don't mean that. My vision blurred as tears trickled down my cheeks. What would I be without her? I'd endured being cut off from my power many times, but to have her leave, of her own free will.

And never come back.

No. Just. No.

Bronagh hissed at me. "I must go. Do as you decide. But make your choice quickly. Before it's too late." And then, she was gone.

Shaylee took over while I was still distracted, leaning out the roots of the tree prison. "Guards!"

Silver-booted feet appeared at eye level through the roots. "Princess."

"I agree to my mother's terms," Shaylee said through my lips. "Take me to her at once."

The roots parted immediately, the ground rising to lift me out of the hole. Shaylee stepped us out onto the grass, even as my eyes fell on Venner.

"He is to come as well." I pulled back control from Shaylee and pointed at the Unseelie lordling. "Or there's no deal." Okay, I was reaching for tiny threads of hope. From the glitter in Venner's eyes, he knew it.

After a very brief whispered conversation with two of his companions, the soldier nodded.

"Very well." The root system of Venner's tree parted, his tall, thin body soon standing next to me. "Come."

Another dozen guards, another trek over white stones, through swaying trees to the happy sound of birds and bubbling water. Except this time, I didn't hear or see any of it. Not while my heart broke over and over with each step.

Despite my desperate brain wracking to the contrary, by the time I was led, head down, before the queen again, hating the sight of her ugly pavilion, her hideous throne, her smiling face, I had nothing new to try.

No last-minute plan. No Syd to save the day.

Nada. Zipperino.

I was about to lose Shaylee and there was nothing I

could do about it.

"You've decided?" Aoilainn leaned forward in her throne, eager, a silken spider weaving threads of lies and falsehood around her. There was a time I thought the vampire Queens evil.

They had nothing on the false beauty and deceit of the Seelie Queen.

Sydlynn, Shaylee sent when I hesitated. *Please, you must let me go.*

I won't, I sent. *But you're welcome to leave. I won't stop you. But I won't help you, either.*

She sighed, hugged me again. *So be it*, she sent.

I looked up, met Aoilainn's eyes, caught a flicker of movement as Bronagh slid onto the dais behind her queen, green gown floating around her. "One condition," I said. "When you have Shaylee in the nasty little trap you've made for your own daughter," let her choke on that one, "I take all of my friends and Venner here with me." I jerked a thumb at the Unseelie lordling.

Aoilainn nodded with her same smile. "Of course."

"Mother." Shaylee spoke for me. "You have proven yourself deceitful. And I tell you now, if you do not let them pass, leave this realm, if anything happens to Sydlynn or her companions before they exit the Gate, I will leave this form you've made me and never again be reborn." Her voice, our voice, shook with her conviction.

Aoilainn's face fell. She'd clearly planned something

diabolical. But faced with her daughter's rebellion, I hoped she had no recourse. Although, I also knew, as the mistress of falsehood, she might be able to trick Shaylee into thinking we were safe when we weren't. But was Aoilainn's revenge worth losing the prize she'd fought for so hard?

The queen finally settled back in her throne with a pout. "Very well," she said. "You have my word of honor, and that of the Sidhe."

Shaylee? I had to know.

She will honor the agreement. She sounded relieved.

There was that much, at least.

"Thalion." Aoilainn waved toward the waiting prince who watched me with his still and quiet eyes. "Retrieve my daughter and return her to us. At last."

Shaylee whispered to me just as Thalion's power touched me. *I love you, too*, she sent. *All of you. Thank you for teaching me to what it means to be strong and brave. I wish things had turned out differently. And if there is a way to do as Bronagh plans, I will try, I swear it. But please, don't risk anything else for me.*

True to my word, I didn't help, but I also didn't hinder. My demon whimpered, huddling inside me while my vampire turned into a coil of sadness and slunk low. The family magic did try to reach for Shaylee, but I held it back as she sent out a wave of love just before she slid free of me. Of us.

chapter twenty seven

Green Sidhe magic flowed from me, a mist of pulsating energy, coming to hover beside me, still connected to my fingertips by the barest touch. It was so strange to feel Shaylee on the outside while I continued to experience our connection.

The mist thickened, turned opaque, the barest features forming in the face, arms and flowing hair, the hem of a dress all undulating as though a strong wind could blow her soul away.

I didn't care who saw my tears as Shaylee lifted her free hand to wave at me, a smile forming on her face, crystal points of light sliding down her soul's cheeks as she, too, wept. I forced myself to watch, even though I just wanted to turn away. She turned and touched the construct her mother created for her, the magic of her essence sliding over the twisted vines and into them.

I held the feeling of her for as long as I could, and it seemed she did the same, not losing the last of our contact until absolutely necessary. I found myself, unknowing I'd moved, standing right next to the created form, my hand holding the writhing wood as the final thread of magic keeping us together snapped with a finality I'd borne only once before.

The night I lost my demon.

At least this time, I had support. My vampire and my demon, the family magic, all of it, there to hold me up, comforting me as I comforted them. My fingers tingled as the vines turned to cool, smooth skin, Shaylee's new flesh squeezing mine before she dropped her hand away. The rest of the construct flowed with life, transforming from a roughly Sidhe shaped woman's form to the body and face I knew so well.

I staggered away from her, suddenly heavy, my earth magic reaching for the ground below us as it seemed the whole of the Sidhe realm settled on my shoulders. My body ached, muscles screaming unhappily, most likely from the fight with Quaid. I figured I'd pay for that one way or another. Thankfully, my vampire's spirit magic soothed my pain enough I could focus.

I looked down at my scruffy sneakers, jeans with the knees covered in dirt, my long, dark hair falling forward over my t-shirt. Softly pink hands with chewed nails resembled nothing even close to the perfection standing in front of me.

I wasn't Shaylee anymore. And she wasn't me.

Worse, the maji magic I'd been in close contact with over the last little while sighed and retreated, no longer answering me when I called to it.

This was very, very bad.

I just couldn't bring myself to worry about the rest of the planes. Not while a gaping hole inside me reminded me with every painful heartbeat, I was no longer whole.

Shaylee's mind reached out and touched mine. It felt wrong to not know her thoughts, not feel what she felt as she spoke in my head.

Let us part with love, she sent. *Always, Sydlynn.*

Always. Even my mental voice choked on the goodbye.

Shaylee turned and, shoulders back and head high, crossed in her flowing stride to join her mother. I watched with growing despair as she turned and stood at Aoilainn's side, one hand on the arm of her mother's throne, Bronagh's emerald gaze locked on the princess, an odd hunger on her face that flashed out to calm after only a moment.

I couldn't muster interest in the advisor's expression.

It was really over.

I snuffled, wiping at my cheeks with the shoulder of my t-shirt, feeling suddenly awkward and uncomfortable in my own body, the last tingle of the ache hanging around to remind me I'd won a fight but lost the battle.

It will take some time to adjust, my vampire sent. *But we* will *adjust*.

She was right. And I didn't have time to stand around feeling sorry for myself. "We did our part," I said, my own voice harsh in the quiet, serene setting. I'd missed it though, and took strength from the sound. "Hand over my friends."

Aoilainn turned from her careful examination of Shaylee and shrugged. "Of course. Off with you, then." The ground around me erupted, figures emerging to sprawl at my feet. Charlotte leaped to her four paws, shaking soil from her fur, snapping and snarling while Galleytrot lurched forward with a vicious howl. I helped Gram to her feet, Fergus beside her, my grandmother's eyes wide as they passed over me, understanding shining in her gaze while Quaid, now dressed as I was in his jeans and shirt, ran his hands through his hair to knock out the clumps of dirt, a deep scowl on his face.

"Hear me, Seelie Queen." Galleytrot's rumbling voice shook the ground beneath me, bringing squeals of fear from the gathered Sidhe, as the sky overhead darkened and dimmed. "You have interfered with happenings beyond your control and will pay the price for your selfishness." Clouds rushed forward, tearing open to send a downpour of rain over the gathered court, a tent of green magic just barely keeping the queen from the soaking she deserved. "When the day comes you need her help," he didn't bother turning to me, his meaning obvious, "when the Brotherhood comes to strip you of your power and destroy your realm, I will not argue with her when she lets you fall."

Aoilainn actually looked a little shaken, but it passed as Galleytrot's next snarl was accompanied by a flash of lightning so close I heard a tree crack and felt the pressure of it against my chest just as a giant crash of thunder broke over us.

I covered my ears with both hands, keeping my feet while many of the remaining Sidhe, soldiers and courtiers alike, fell to the ground, clutching at each other.

Aoilainn stood, pointing at Galleytrot with one shaking hand. "Hound," she said, "your power is limited here. Bring Gwynn before me if you plan to threaten and perhaps I'll listen."

"I have no doubt he and the Wild Hunt will come to you some day," Galleytrot said. "And I will take great joy carrying you to the darkness in my jaws."

She paled, spinning on Thalion. "Escort this rabble to the Gate," she said, "and ensure they never again return to my realm." Her eyes fixed on mine, though the seed of worry haunted the depths of her gaze. "Under penalty of death."

With freaking pleasure.

I wanted to be strong as Thalion stepped forward,

several soldiers hesitantly joining him, to escort us out. He bowed to me, offered his hand, but I ignored him. I turned my back on the queen, on the court, on everything. But no matter how strong I intended to be, I couldn't help myself.

As we crossed the small bridge over the stream, leaving the clearing and the pavilion behind, I cast one last look back.

And found Shaylee watching me go.

chapter twenty eight

I stumbled a few times, trying my best to stay focused while my body fought to understand what had changed. No more the casual grace of Shaylee's form, or the speed, either. I struggled to keep up, forcing the others to slow. Only Quaid seemed to have the same issues.

"The armor must have added something extra," he said as he walked beside me. "I feel like the whole world is sitting on me."

Not to mention the fact I'd shrunk. Okay, not really. But everyone else seemed so tall, their Sidhe forms towering over me. Charlotte's wolf head was at level with mine and Galleytrot looked like an elephant. Amazing what an extra six inches could do, once they were taken away.

Gram paced along beside me on my left, Venner just ahead with Fergus. I kept an eye on Venner as best I could, but between the ache in my soul and the adaptation to this new reality, I could barely keep from collapsing in a sobbing heap for a few minutes.

Which would turn into a few hours, I had no doubt.

No crying. That was for later.

My alter egos were quiet, their sadness not really helping much, but I could hardly blame them. At least the family magic was content to wrap around and hold me tight, as though welcoming me back though I hadn't gone anywhere. And the earth magic I had access to kept me anchored. Unlike a normal human, I wouldn't be trapped here if I tried to leave. Without earth magic to help me find my way, even if the queen did fulfill her side of the bargain, I would end up wandering here forever looking for a way out.

That didn't mean I could waste time, though. "Thalion." He turned to look back at me. "We still need to find Ameline." No way she'd left yet. Or had she? I had no idea, really. Maybe she'd found what she searched for and was long gone.

That would be just my luck. Go through all of this for nothing. I was starting to wish I'd just set up camp outside the Gate and waited for her to come back through. And the Sidhe realm be damned if she did any damage.

One look to my left showed the advancing cloudbank had grown in size, a black line of churning storm fury.

Galleytrot raised some weather, but this resembled the full brunt of the Wild Hunt. Which made me gasp and clutch at my chest.

She wouldn't. "Galleytrot." I breathed his name.

He towered over me as he turned his great head and met my eyes. "What's wrong?"

I pointed at the approaching storm. "Could Ameline have raised the Wild while we were fighting the Queen?"

He stopped, spinning to watch the rippling mass of clouds. "No," he said. "This isn't my lord's work. It's something else, something older, Syd. Tied to the Creators."

The maji. "So she's figuring it out," I said, heavy and dull.

"Perhaps," he said. "Though I doubt it. The maji would not destroy. Whatever she's stirring, it goes against the power of the Creators."

"Which means, she still hasn't found what she needs." Gram's hand took mine, squeezing gently, her flawless face frowning. How had I thought we looked alike? Her Sidhe form was so stunningly gorgeous, my normal body a bit of a wreck. "So stop being an idiot, girl, and focus."

"We must speak to my king." Venner stopped too, turning to Galleytrot, ignoring the flash of worry on Thalion's face.

"You just want to go home." I aimed a bitter mental curse his way. "You're welcome, jerktard."

After all this, he was the only one getting what he wanted, wasn't he?

I was actually surprised to see the concern on his face. "You may think little of me, Sydlynn," he said. "But I am aware of how dangerous Ameline is." He shook his head, silver hair rippling in its silver cuffs. "When I think how she manipulated me, I'm still amazed." Arrogant ass. Still. "And if she is loose in our realm," his eyes drifted to the storm gathering, closer now than when we'd first arrived, "my King must be warned. Especially if the Seelie Queen won't listen to reason."

That was a clear shot at Thalion, though the prince didn't argue or defend his ruler.

"I have been a fool," Venner said, holding out his hands toward me. "My only wish has been to return home. And I have done things I'm not proud of to make that heart's longing come to pass." He bowed his head to Fergus. "But believe me, now that I'm home again, making sure this place is safe has to be my priority."

Part of me softened. Understood. When I'd been trapped on Demonicon, thanks to my demon grandmother's need to manipulate Dad, I vowed to do anything and everything I could to get home. And while I'd chosen not to betray or manipulate people to get the job done, I'd only had a few day's worth of trying.

What would I have finally sunk to, what depths, to go home?

And was I really any different than Venner?

Sigh. I hated it when the bad guys crossed the line. It made my job all that much harder.

"Okay," I said, while Gram nodded. "We'll go talk to the King."

Thalion swayed before speaking. "Her Majesty ordered me to escort you to the Gate."

I was on him in a flash, in his beautiful face towering over me. Thalion didn't move or flinch as I jabbed him in the chest with one index finger.

"If you really love Shaylee," I snarled, "you'll make sure her crazy ass mother doesn't end up killing everyone from pure selfishness."

Thalion's hands settled on my shoulders, gently, as he bowed his head. "The Shaylee I love doesn't exist anymore," he whispered. "You've changed her. Though I don't mind the changes." His lips lifted to a little smile. "But her heart was never mine, I know that now. And my queen's duplicity puts us all at risk." Thalion released me, squaring his shoulders. "I will lead you to the Unseelie border."

Talk about shock me down to the ground. "Thank you." Maybe he wasn't such a bad guy after all. And worthy of Shaylee, in the end.

I turned to Venner, eyes narrowed, still not trusting him. Not completely. "You betray me, tall and shiny, and I'll kick your Unseelie ass. Hear me?"

He reached out, shared a scrap of his power, the Sidhe magic taking some of the weight from my body. "I do," he said, eyes twinkling, but not with humor. "Have no fear. For as long as Ameline is our common enemy, I am your ally." Venner's jaw clenched. "No one betrays me."

That was honest for someone like him. Truce, until we found and defeated Ameline.

And then all bets were off.

ChAPTER TWENTY NINE

Like most of the Sidhe realm, what seemed like an impossibly long journey from one place to the next took almost no time at all. I just considered asking Thalion how long it would take to reach the border after setting out again, heading toward the storm—of course we were—when the air itself seemed to sigh and shift, the sky dulling. A thin, wavering line of green fire appeared in the grass, separating where we stood from the continued expanse of ground. I almost asked why it hadn't looked like this before and rolled my eyes instead.

More glamour. I was getting very sick of my eyes lying to me.

At least the other side of the magical barrier looked more ordinary. Made me wonder if the Unseelie King was less into the fake presentation or if he'd grunge things up just to push the limits. I'd heard only bad things about the dark court. While the Seelie were tricksy and more than a little arrogant, all tales I'd heard of the Unseelie made me wince. Monsters welcome. Though, from my experience with Venner and my encounter with Aoilainn, I was beginning to wonder who were the real monsters here.

The Unseelie lordling stepped forward, face eager, his magic sliding around him as he reached out to the line of fire. Thalion stared over the flickering line of flames as two stone posts rose from the ground, pushing their way to the surface in answer to Venner's rising hands. The columns continued to grow, slender, carved rock finally forming an archway that sealed together at the top with the sound of grinding gravel.

More magic flared along the seal, running down the columns, lighting the carvings until it dove down into the ground. The fire parted, leaving a doorway through the barrier between one kingdom and the next.

Venner turned and saluted Thalion and, to my surprise, the prince saluted back. "Be well, Your Highness," Venner said. "I've never wished you malice."

Thalion's smile was thin. "Just my queen. I understand." His eyes dropped to me. "More now than ever."

I wondered how painful his education was. How many years had Thalion believed in his queen? Only to have that loyalty shattered thanks to the princess he loved.

Yeah, I could still feel sympathy. Shocking.

A touch of his power straightened my shoulders as Thalion echoed Venner's offering, his magic meshing with my earth ability.

"Thanks," I said, really meaning it. "We could really use your help, you know."

Thalion nodded, but the slumped set of his shoulders told me what he was going to say before he said it. "I cannot." He touched my hair with his fingertips, drawing a low growl from Charlotte and a protective sway from Quaid. "I must obey my queen, even now."

He turned, eyes landing on Fergus. "You will join them, old friend?"

I never considered the fact Liam's grandfather was Thalion's buddy. Or that the prince had any kind of friends, for that matter. I hated underestimating people.

Hated it.

Fergus smiled and bowed to the prince. "My grandson, your Gatekeeper, needs my help. And I can't let him down."

Thalion reached out and took Fergus's hand. "Take good care," he said before turning and leaving us there, his long legs covering a large amount of ground quickly. I knew he was aided by magic because, within half a dozen strides, he disappeared from view.

Time to face the music. I spun back, eyes running over the low line of black clouds on the other side of the barrier. Maybe it was a sign Ameline was in the Unseelie court?

"She acts against my king." Venner's melodic voice came out as a growl. "She must have some influence with Aoilainn and fears Odhran. Why else would she focus the storm in the Unseelie kingdom?"

I figured there was a flaw in his logic, but let him have his belief. "Let's just go talk to your king," I said. "Maybe he'll be more helpful in tracking Ameline." I reached out for the witch even as Venner turned and strode through the archway, knowing it wasn't likely I'd feel her even if she was here. Especially now that I didn't have access to Shaylee's soul. If Ameline was still hiding behind a Sidhe reincarnation, even Liam's, without Shaylee to track her I was out of luck.

Or was I? I turned to Galleytrot as Quaid and Gram, Fergus behind them, followed Venner through the arching stone.

Can you track Ameline here? Why hadn't I thought to ask him originally? Probably because the idea was to talk to the queen then go find the evil little witch. I realized now I should have reversed the order of my priorities.

Galleytrot chuffed softly, Charlotte closing in on my right side, him on my left as the three of us approached the crossing. The others stood on the other side, waiting, watching us. So far, so safe. A moment of nerves gripped me as I considered this could be a trap. Venner could still be working with Ameline.

Galleytrot's answer to my question told me we were out of options. *I've been trying*, he sent. *As has Charlotte*. The big wolf tossed her head in agreement. *But the glamour and the pull of Sidhe magic mask everything*.

So we go to the Unseelie, I said. *And see if the king is a smarter cookie than his counterpart*. Fingers crossed. Toes. Every part of me I could manage.

Galleytrot grunted. *I hold out hope*, he sent. *But it's slim*.

Well, I'd take it.

I felt her power before I could take the step that would carry me from one realm to the next and paused, turning back as Bronagh raced over the hill and to my side, her flowing green gown a rippling wave around her.

"Sydlynn," she said as she came to a halt beside me, eyes huge as she looked over the barrier. "What are you doing?"

"Looking for help," I said.

"The queen will find out." She clutched her hands to her chest. "She will punish Shaylee for your duplicity."

I hadn't considered that. "I can't just leave without trying to stop Ameline," I said. "I just can't."

Bronagh nodded at last, a heavy sigh slumping her graceful form. "I understand," she said. "I will do what I can to hold off Aoilainn's wrath."

I had to go back for Shaylee. This was ridiculous. Maybe now that my friends were safe on the Unseelie side…

Bronagh must have sensed what I was thinking because she straightened. "Go," she said. "I will care for Shaylee."

"This could work," I said. "We could free her now while the others are safe."

"And then what?" Bronagh's long, dark hair whispered as she shook her head. "The Gate is on the Seelie side."

Right. "So I send the others home." Why hadn't I thought of that? "Get Shaylee then talk to the king of the Unseelie."

Bronagh grasped my shoulders in her long-fingered hands, the buzz of her magic blocked from me now that I wasn't Sidhe anymore. "You must trust me," she said. "Taking care of Shaylee is my responsibility now. And I won't fail her."

Something stirred in me. A memory. I'd heard those words before. Desperate need made me crumble a little.

"You promise you'll bring her to the Gate?" There was still that hope, though it sounded like Shaylee was done with me, no matter if her mother relented or not.

Bronagh smiled and nodded. "I can absolutely guarantee I will bring her to the Gate," she said, "and she will cross over again to your plane. Take heart in that fact."

It was all I had to cling to. "Thank you."

She laughed. "No," she said. "Thank you. Now go. And do what you can to stir the king to action."

Why was she thanking me? The Sidhe were weird.

A deep breath and a whispered plea to the powers that be and I left Bronagh there, turning to step through the archway into the Unseelie kingdom.

chapter thirty

I'm not sure what I was expecting. Thunderclaps and lightning and doom coming down on me, maybe. Instead, I rubbed my arms against the subtle chill in the air, feet sliding over dry grass and onto a graveled path. I turned to look back, over the shining land the queen maintained as her reality, Bronagh already gone from view, before spinning back to compare.

Not dismal, not really. Just duller, unglamoured. Ordinary. Trees dotted the distance, a riverbank not far away, likely the same one running past the queen's palace. Its banks looked rocky, not the shining white stone I was used to now, but gray and laced with darkness and light. A real river.

So the king did like things based in reality. This could work to my advantage after all.

"What did she want?" Quaid fell in beside me.

"Nothing." I sighed and shrugged. "Let's just keep moving."

Venner's beaming smile almost made me laugh, would have if I wasn't in such a horrible state of mind. He looked like a kid who'd just been granted his fondest wish. And while he didn't seem so shining, so polished, he still appeared unearthly, smooth skin now showing pores, imperfections. He looked like he had back on my plane.

Even better.

Gram still appeared like me, only much more so, her perfection faded, too, along with her height. We were now shoulder-to-shoulder, though she still wore her ridiculous gown. Charlotte snorted, looking down at her paws, shrunk to a more normal size, though still large enough to give an ordinary wolf pause. And Galleytrot was Galleytrot, not pachyderm dog.

Good enough.

The sky began to darken as I looked up, but not from storm clouds. "Night?"

Venner nodded, still happy, but settling as he turned toward the bank in the distance. "My lord prefers it," he said. "Come, it's not far now."

The further we walked—though not far, since the king seemed to like manipulating space himself—the darker it became until it felt like full night. No moon shone over us, the sky more silver than black, plenty of light from what felt like a night sky. A very odd sensation that made me feel like I was in a dream.

Creepy.

The light cast everything in cold silver, from the grass to the water of the river and the leaves of the trees we approached. I thought the tunnel to the queen's palace was dark when we'd arrived. This passage through the bending forest was positively pitch.

More creepy. I called up my demon's night-vision, but no luck. She snarled in frustration. For whatever reason, her enhanced senses couldn't cut through the black.

So the king liked changing reality after all.

Good to know.

Venner's steps didn't waver as he carried on forward toward the gaping hole in the trees. I followed with a heavy heart, wondering what mess I was getting us into this time. Only Gram's fingers wound around mine and Charlotte's steady presence at my side kept my chin up.

Galleytrot and Quaid fell behind us. I could feel their magic reaching out, keeping watch and kicked myself for not thinking of such protections in the first place.

You have enough on your mind, Quaid sent to me when I reached for him to apologize. *Let us watch over you.*

Well. Um. Okay then.

Enter throat lump. And all kinds of guilt.

Light flickered into life as we set foot under the trees, flashing fireflies the size of my hand creating a strobe effect quickly giving me a headache. When one flew too near I realized it wasn't a lightning bug at all, but a tiny Fey, her face all sharp angles, body glowing on and off as she floated by my cheek to study me.

I figured it would be rude to swat at her and let her fill her boots.

It was quickly apparent the Unseelie court was a mimic of its shining counterpart, only dressed in doom and cold metal. By the time we crossed the low bridge over the rushing stream and into the clearing beyond, I was feeling dark side deja vu.

The lawn overflowed with watching eyes, glowing green in the darkness, looming above, lurking below. Shivers ran through me, visions of horror movie endings running through my head. The scary music played and I was the stupid girl reaching for the basement door.

I tried to peer through the dark and make out solid shapes, catching nightmare glimpses only. Instead of sparkling Sidhe with their beautiful faces and bodies and clothing, the space flooded with Fey of all shapes and sizes, each of them wreathed in shadows they seemed to carry with them. Hulking brutes with flattened faces and skin like stone hunkered near the tree line while more tiny fairies flew about, some glowing, some carrying that pure black with them.

Something rumbled and slithered near my feet, making me jump with a little meep. I seriously had to get a grip.

The only things keeping me moving were momentum and Venner's lack of concern. Not that I trusted him, really. But we hadn't been pounced on and eaten whole yet, so I'd give the Unseelie Fey the benefit of the doubt.

For now.

As we drew nearer the center of the clearing, it became easier to see, light appearing from under the dais where the thrones sat. I'm not sure illumination made things much better.

Meira and I used to hold flashlights under our chins and try to scare each other.

Yeah. That times a gazillion.

The underlighting told me one thing, though. The Unseelie king wasn't against a show of his own. And despite the horrible shades cast by the white glow, throwing giant shadows against the trees, I relaxed a little.

He was trying to scare us. Really scary people? They didn't have to try.

Right at the foot of the throne platform's stairs hovered a fair share of Sidhe who looked like Venner, tall and slim, long-haired and lovely, but they were outnumbered by the grunting, knobby, animal-like or purely ugly who made up the balance of the shadow-wreathed attendees.

On a black marble throne on a tall dais, his own pavilion arching over him, the king of the Unseelie watched our approach with half-lidded eyes. The Fey woman beside him, her lean form wrapped in tight black leather, bobbed one foot over her crossed knee, head tilted to the side, a little smile pulling the corner of her mouth.

I thought Aoilainn and her Seelie were tall.

The king had to be twenty feet at least, with shoulders wider than the business end of a tractor trailer.

Yikes.

Venner came to a halt before his king and swept into an elaborate bow while the gathered Fey fell still.

"Your Majesty," he said. "I have come home at last."

The crowd erupted into rude laughter and noises, shuffling and shifting, closing in on us further. I held my ground, keeping my calm as best I could as my fear rose. Okay. So maybe the show wasn't that easy to brush off. They really did give me goosebumps to rival any Hollywood horror flick. Partly because I had no way of knowing if I looked like an ally or dinner to most of the court.

Though if they tried to eat me, I swore I'd do everything I could to make sure they'd end up with a wicked case of indigestion.

My eyes followed the towering spires, high over the trees and I felt a pang of disdain break through no matter my fear. Seriously? No originality.

It took a moment for quiet to return. Rather than

silencing his people, the king let them chatter themselves into stillness before he spoke.

"Venemeth." The ground under my feet shook from that one word, my whole body trembling with the force of the king's massive voice. "I seem to recall I promised to crush your soul if I ever saw you again."

Mostly, after the first few words, all I heard was BOOM BOOM MUTTER GROWL. Though I caught enough of it to piece the intent together. I fought not to dig my fingers in my ears and shake them, my head ringing.

When my hearing cleared, it was to laughter. One of the tiny, glowing Fey rushed forward and pulled on Venner's hair. The lordling ignored everyone but his king as my heart beat faster.

He wanted to what? I shot a tight thought to Venner. *You failed to mention your king hates your guts.*

What had he gotten us into?

"My king," Venner said, still smiling, smooth and polished as if his ruler hadn't just threatened his very existence. "Certain risks to my home have come to light. I rushed to your side to warn you before it is too late."

Odhran's gaze settled on me a moment, then Gram. "You bring me witches," he said, voice dropping in volume enough I could make him out at least, though it seemed my very bones vibrated in time with the pressure of the sounds. "An old Gatekeeper." His massive brow furrowed as he looked at Fergus, but he continued. "A wolf. And a hound of the Wild Hunt. I'm assuming this threat you mention has to do with them?"

"Yes, Your Majesty." Venner turned and gestured to me. "My companions seek the threat right now."

I guessed that was my cue. My knees wobbled a little as I stepped forward, an aftereffect of the shaking in my bones. And fear.

Yeah. Fear. I wasn't whole anymore, was I? The power I'd used against Aoilainn, the magic of the maji? I didn't have access any longer. So fear.

Sucked so much.

"Your Majesty," I said, pulling on my Mom diplomat memories. "My name is Sydlynn Hayle. And I think your realm has a problem."

He remained silent, as did his court, as I quickly filled him in on Ameline and our encounter with Aoilainn. The Unseelie queen snorted, as loud as a gunshot, when I mentioned her counterpart, but didn't say anything.

I wasn't sure how much to tell him and ended up spilling a longer story than I intended. The oppressive feel of his presence, the weight of the darkness and the growing feeling I had of my own tiny and fragile nature had me on edge and decidedly vulnerable, the most vulnerable I'd been in a very long time.

So, probably babbling, but needing him to hear me and understand, I brought up the trouble at Harvard with the vampire cult as well as my grandmother's loss on Demonicon and Ameline's present gambit, the risk to Liam's life.

I felt like I'd talked forever by the time I wound down, more than a little embarrassed by my verbal gushing, finally ending with the loss of Shaylee. Tears stung my eyes and, though I swore I wouldn't cry in front of the Unseelie king and his smirking queen, by the time I finished they both seemed intent and serious.

And… smaller?

Odhran exchanged a look with the Fey woman beside him. "Niamh," he said, his voice fading to a more normal level as his body shrank, throne too, until he seemed the same size as Venner. "What say you, my wife?"

She sat back, her own body now shrunk to manageable proportions, chewing her bottom lip. "When you first entered our presence," she said, "and I saw the Gatekeeper, I thought the girl had returned."

My ears perked while I mentally kicked myself for falling for the old growing trick. Dad had done it, Ahbi. Even Galleytrot. I knew better than to be intimidated by such magic. And yet, I was Shayleeless. So I cut myself some slack and focused. "Girl, Your Majesty?"

The queen bobbed her head. "Not long ago, one wearing that exact face and carrying Gate power came to us."

I glanced at Fergus who first seemed startled, then

angry.

"My grandson's face," he said.

Odhran's eyes drifted over Fergus before he nodded to his queen. "Indeed," he said. "She claimed to be a Keeper, but she simply wore the stolen form. His power was not part of her."

"Unlike the one with you," Niamh said. "He is true Sidhe."

Fergus bowed. "We seek that one and the power she stole, Your Majesties," he said.

This little chat was much more helpful than our last one. Awesome. Hope surged inside me. "May I ask how you saw through her so easily?" If I could figure that out, I could use it to my advantage. If Ameline was still here.

The king stood. "You intrigue us, witch girl," he said. "Come. We shall feast. And talk further."

Great. More eating. Though I was hungry, fair enough. "We're on a bit of a time crunch, here."

The king shrugged and turned from me, arm linking with his queen. "We dine," he said. "You may stay or go. Either way."

Grumble, mumble.

Unlike Aoilainn's court, the main clearing wasn't host to the feast. I followed the royal couple, Sidhe of all shapes and sizes falling back into shadows as the path opened up past the pavilion dais and to another open area, already equipped with a table, chairs and a vast meal.

My stomach grumbled while my mind churned.

Traitor.

Venner selected a seat and sat as though he'd never left while one of the floating, glowing Fey guided me to sit next to the king. My last feast with the Sidhe had led to lost time and Shaylee's thralling. I could only stay alert and hope Odhran had better intentions than Aoilainn.

"You asked how we saw through the intruder's falsehood," the king said as he sipped a glass of deep red wine. At least the table was well lit, though I had to force myself to keep my eyes down or on him and not let them skim the gathered Unseelie who hunkered around the edges of the light as though coming into it would harm them. "We are Unseelie." He tapped the back of my hand with one fingertip. "It is our nature to see past the glamour of others."

Loud and clear. And gave me the seed of an idea, though the thought of it made my stomach churn and my mind whisper, *How could you?* I shoved it off, hope growing even more. "Is she still here, this girl?"

The queen laughed, a spoon full of something sparkling hovering near her mouth. "No," Niamh said. "We sent her off. She and her pathetic attempt to manipulate us."

I was liking these Unseelie more and more by the moment. Especially when the whole court rumbled with good humor. Not so scary now, these monstrous Fey.

Not hiding from the light, were they, but only wanting to hear, to learn why we were in their territory. At least at the moment. I had no illusions they were on my side. But they hadn't given in to Ameline.

"May I ask," time to be polite, Syd, "what she was after?"

I was wondering when you were going to get to the point, Gram growled in my head.

"One of our souls," the king said. "So she could be full Sidhe."

"I'm assuming you turned her down, my king?" Venner's smile flashed, wicked.

"Naturally," Odhran said. "Our souls are not lightly shared with others."

Which meant my idea might not work out after all. Still, it couldn't hurt to ask.

Well, not much. I wasn't sure my heart would forgive me.

"As I said," I toyed with the food on my plate, the smell divine, but my appetite turned to ashes in my mouth. "I've lost my Sidhe soul. And I need her."

The king didn't speak. Not a good sign.

"You've heard of the maji?" I met his eyes, knowing I took a big risk. But when Gram didn't protest, kick me or tell me I was being an idiot for sharing too much, I went on after Odhran nodded. "Well, when I'm whole, I'm one of them." Okay, not quite accurate. And from the skeptical look on the royal's faces, they weren't buying it.

"There's something coming," I said, opening my heart and my knowledge to the king and queen, letting them feel my other magicks, after which they exchanged a quick glance before their suspicion faded. "A battle, led by darkness." Maybe not the best of terminology considering where I was, but it was the most apt description I could come up with. "The sorcerers."

Niamh hissed softly, leaned toward me across her husband. "Yes," she said, intensity in her black eyes, flickers of green Sidhe fire flashing there. "I know of this. Have felt its portents." She sat back then, gaze narrowed. "It's possible it's you she spoke of."

She? I shelved that question for the moment. "Then you understand," I said. "Why I need a soul." Shudder. So. Wrong. "Without Sidhe magic, I can't do what I have to do." Fulfill my damned destiny and all that crap.

My other magicks protested instantly at the thought, but I had to ask. Didn't I?

Had to.

The queen's sudden sympathy almost made me cry in frustration, because I felt her magic's answer before she spoke. "While we could supply you with what you ask for," she said, "the soul wouldn't be what you need, Sydlynn. Only she who is part of you can fill that gap and make you whole."

Okay. I knew that.

We all do, my vampire whispered while my demon whimpered.

I bowed my head a moment before nodding. "Thank you," I said. "You're right." When I met her eyes again, she was still smiling, but with warmth. "Do you know where the intruder girl went, Your Majesty?" I could only guess. Ameline had to be back with the Seelie.

"We chased her to our border," Niamh said while the gathered court rumbled their pleasure, "and haven't seen her since." She smiled at her husband, kindness vanished. Her expression was now more like Venner's. "Perhaps she convinced that ridiculous Aoilainn to accept her offer."

Galleytrot muttered a growl. "You were wise to turn her away, great king, wise queen," he rumbled while the gathered Fey actually fell back just a fraction. So they were afraid of my big friend, were they? Good to know. "No pact you could make with Ameline would have ended well for your people."

She has to be in Aoilainn's court, Gram sent to me. *And is probably the reason the queen refused to listen to reason.*

I shuddered at the thought. Could she have managed to take over the queen? That would be a disaster.

No, Gram sent. *But someone close to her... yes. Possibly.*

I thought of Thalion.

Stopped.

Cursed in my head so loud even my demon protested,

as I pieced together a hungry look with a familiar phrase and a thank you I hadn't earned.

Bronagh.

Of course.

I rose from the table, bowing quickly to the king and queen. "Thank you," I said. "It's a relief to know some of those in the Sidhe realm are willing to pay attention when their people are in danger."

Before the royal pair could protest our leaving, one of the small, glowing Fey streaked across the clearing and landed on the king's shoulder. I held still, watched as Odhran's face stilled, turned dark and, finally flashed with rage before he waved the tiny form off.

"It seems our paths are one, Sydlynn Hayle," he said, rising from the table with his queen at his side. His court took that as some kind of signal, wandering off with tweets, chirps, mumbles and grunts, heavy footfalls and flashing wings the song of their departure.

The king seemed less perfect up close, his wife the same, though both had the angular beauty of the Sidhe.

"You were received here because I was curious about you," he said. "Have been since a Gatekeeper failed to answer the knock not so long ago." It felt like forever to me since Liam and I saved the world, but I didn't have as many years under my belt as the king. "Your name has been whispered among the Fey, in case you didn't know."

Gossip? Not sure I was happy about that. "I'm only

here to make things right." Best they both knew that in no uncertain terms.

Why was I still here talking to them? I really, really had to go and find out if I was right.

"I have looked past you and into your soul," Niamh said reaching out one hand to touch my cheek, quieting the urgency I felt to hunt down Bronagh and tear open the glamour around her to see if another face lived beneath it. A hated face. "And I believe your heart is pure."

Well, I wasn't so sure about pure, exactly, especially since I was presently considering all the violent things I would do to Ameline when I caught up with her. But I wasn't about to argue with the queen when it might help my case. For the first time since I arrived in the Sidhe realm, I was actually feeling some real optimism.

"We know a battle is coming," Odhran said. "Signs of the approaching conflict are everywhere, if one is willing to pay attention." A clear jab at Aoilainn. I agreed with him. "A maji has come to Niamh in her dreams, telling of a witch with the heart of a Sidhe princess, the soul of a demon and the blood of a vampire. One who would come to us for our help."

The "she" Niamh mentioned, the question I'd waited to pursue. Iepa. Had to be the same maji. She'd taken interest in me, the one who told me about this destiny of mine. And while I wished she was wrong, there was no use fighting it now.

They could have just told me in the first place.

"I've lost my Sidhe soul," I said. Again with the prickling tears and the rising grief, fed by the anxious need to rush back to the Seelie court and test my theory about Bronagh. No time for sadness, Syd. Later. "But not my sense of duty." That much was true. "Ameline is my priority."

Again the king and queen met each other's eyes before they nodded in tandem.

"Agreed," they said. The king's jaw jumped. "We feel that same duty, at least to our people. I've just received word an army of Seelie warriors gathers at our border and their queen is among them."

Oops. That had to be bad.

Niamh's smile held bite. "It appears we're coming with you."

CHAPTER THIRTY ONE

It didn't take long for the Unseelie king and queen to assemble a large party for the ride back to the barrier between kingdoms. I was a little surprised they were so willing to step up and knew my cynicism came from dealing with Aoilainn. I promised myself if Shaylee's mother was acting like a total bitch because Ameline had somehow influenced her, I'd give her the benefit of the doubt later.

I wasn't holding my breath.

Oh, yes. And when I said ride? I didn't mean horses. I was quite firmly hoisted onto the back of one of the giant stone Fey, settled on his right shoulder while Gram was placed next to me with lots of space for the two of us. Quaid hitched along with the Sidhe's partner, who I supposed was an attractive troll with her lovely weeds for hair. I caught myself laughing as she handed Quaid a flower with her gigantic fingers.

Someone has a crush on you.

Quaid shot me a glare while Fergus settled next to him with a big grin on his face.

Oh, shut up, Quaid muttered.

I looked down, a very long way down, feeling my fear of heights trigger, to the sight of Charlotte pacing nervously at the giant's feet.

"Careful where you walk, please," I said directly in his ear. Stone ground together as he turned his head to fix me with his glowing green eyes. Well, eye. And even looking up at that huge orb made me dizzy.

"Of course," he said in the gentlest voice I'd ever heard. "I'm always cautious."

Guilt welled up as I patted his cheek. "Thanks, big guy."

His smile was filled with wooden teeth and moss. Gross, yes. But I'd take him over his weight in Seelie Fey any day.

The king and queen mounted a chariot pulled by four huge dogs, sleek to Galleytrot's shagginess. They whimpered and bowed to him as he walked past. A call to the team and they were off, giant transportation striding along, keeping easy pace.

Charlotte and Galleytrot ran along with them, the wolf keeping up, so I didn't worry. Not to mention the fact my giant friend was as careful as he claimed, eyes roving the ground before him to watch for obstacles and the stray chasing bodywere.

I looked back over my shoulder at the vast column of Unseelie following us and caught myself grinning. I had no idea what the king and queen had planned, but it looked pretty spectacular from up here.

The barrier appeared, flames licking the grass. And a shining army stood beyond it.

Aoilainn was here. That couldn't be good. But at least it saved us having to call for her.

While I tried to figure out her plans, my eyes traveling over the vast silver army behind her, I felt my heart fall. Yes, the Unseelie looked mighty. But rag-tag, in comparison to the seeming endless sea of silver and gold clad soldiers Aoilainn had at her back.

All of a sudden, I didn't feel so confident.

The chariot stopped just before the barrier, the dogs yapping and whining as they settled on their haunches. I held tight to the giant's thumb as he set Gram and I gently on the grass beside Odhran and Niamh. I took a moment to look up and smile, patting his hand in thanks. He smiled in return before standing to tower over all of us, his shadow the darkness of the Unseelie kingdom.

Quaid joined me, Fergus at his side with Charlotte at my feet and Galleytrot on Gram's right. A solid line, if ever there was one.

Thalion stood beside the queen, his face wreathed in

worry. While Aoilainn wept and wrung her hands before lunging at the barrier, stabbing her finger at me.

"Where is she?" The Seelie queen collapsed a little before her rage and terror returned. "What have you done with my daughter?"

The army of shining Fey behind her shifted, answering her emotions, gathering to attack.

Um, what?

Oh. Crap. Shaylee.

"Return my child," Aoilainn screamed, her beauty fading in the face of her rage, "or I will take her from you by force."

"You will do no such thing," Odhran said while my heart sped up so fast I thought it would leap from my chest and go looking for my Sidhe princess without me. "Sydlynn is under my protections and that of the Unseelie kingdom." Wow. That was huge. I didn't have time to thank him or question his motives as he went on. "Harming her means war between us."

Was it just me or did Niamh look like that would be okay with her? I liked the Unseelie queen more and more.

"I should have known you would be part of this," Aoilainn spat at Odhran. "You've wanted dominion over all the Sidhe since our creation. If you think stealing my daughter's soul will win you anything, you've made your last mistake, monster king of darkness."

I could feel the fury writhing from Odhran, but he

seemed in better control of himself than his Seelie counterpart.

Than I was at the moment.

"And if you think ruling the Sidhe is my goal, you're a fool. A bigger fool than I ever thought." He sighed, shook his head, long black hair a wave of darkness around him as power crackled toward the barrier. "It's time to stop being so selfish, Aoilainn, and start listening."

She snarled and looked like she was about to counter when his power snapped like lightning, winning her silence. "I have been warning you for some time," he said. "There is danger coming, and we must be ready. Work together if we would defeat our foe. Are you so glamoured by your own short sightedness you can't feel it?"

The queen didn't respond.

"What happened to Shaylee?" I needed to know. My fear for her almost consumed me as it rose and swelled and devoured everything else.

Aoilainn's anger returned as she snapped her fingers. Two soldiers brought the body forward, but I could tell it no longer held Shaylee, merely a shell in her shape, already beginning to revert to vegetation. Cracks formed in her skin, scaly bark rising from the hem of her illusionary gown. I choked on a cry, my hand pressed to my open mouth at the sight.

Shaylee was gone.

Where was my Sidhe soul?

chapter Thirty Two

I didn't think, didn't pause, just reached out, searching for Ameline. This had to be her doing. Desperation drove my magic over the barrier and into Seelie territory. I almost didn't make it across, not until Thalion's cool power caught mine and pulled me across.

Girl. Gram's mental voice slashed across my mind. *You're looking for the wrong person.*

Gasp.

Right.

Shaylee. *But Galleytrot said the perpetual magic makes everything muddied.* Here I was arguing against the course of action I'd already set in motion.

Your soul knows the difference, Gram sent, her Sidhe soul's power giving me a boost. *Go find the princess.*

"I don't have your daughter," I snarled at Aoilainn while my mind, tied to Gram and Thalion, tracked back

257

toward the Seelie palace, searching for the touch of my Sidhe princess.

Yes. Mine. And the queen be damned.

I think she knew that right from the start because the moment I spoke, Aoilainn seemed to crumple. "Find her," she wailed. "Bring her back to me and anything you've ever dreamed of is yours."

"Oh, I'm going to find her," I said. "But you're not getting anywhere near her. Ever again. And you don't have a thing I want."

There. Just a hint, a subtle trace under Aoilainn's constant control. I felt Shaylee. And my heart soared.

But wait. Hang on. She wasn't where I felt her. Just an echo, an after-touch of magic. My demon sniffed along the trail, whipping us back toward the river, the valley, the cobbled road.

The Gate.

And there, at the edge of Sidhe territory, I finally felt her at last. Not Shaylee. No.

Ameline.

She had Shaylee.

I hissed at the queen, slashing the air with my magic, fury boiling over as I let my gathered powers out. She thought the storm looming behind me wasn't a threat? Fine, I'd threaten her.

"You stupid, selfish, blind old fairy." It was the best I could manage. I was lucky I could speak past the spitting rage consuming me. "You let in Ameline. And she stole Shaylee from both of us."

Aoilainn blanched, body trembling. "No," she said. "You're lying." She shrugged her shoulders as though to shed my words. "I had no idea this witch you mention was in my realm."

She was just arrogant and shortsighted enough I believed her, though I watched her blanch after admitting she wasn't all knowing, all powerful. "You're the Queen of the Seelie," I said. "It's your job to know."

She stared at me with a blank expression.

"Tell me," I snarled. "Where is your beloved Bronagh, Queen Aoilainn?"

Thalion's frown and quick look around told me everything I needed to know.

"She fooled you," I said with so much bitterness my throat hurt. "She fooled all of us." Bronagh with her kindness, her support. Convincing Shaylee leaving was the only way, that we could get her back once Aoilainn became complacent.

Ameline.

I was the biggest fool of all.

"Someone find her." Aoilainn's order came out as a thin whisper. Thalion nodded quickly, eyes meeting mine, our minds still linked. I followed him as he ran, attached to his magic through the gift he shared, covering the ground with him mentally while Gram turned, our connection humming with power, and gestured, a large, shimmering image appearing before us all.

We saw through Thalion's eyes, even the queen's locked on the view, as he plunged down the path through the trees to the clearing. The palace. Raced across the little bridge to the spiral staircase and up, up through the spires until he reached the level he was looking for.

He didn't slow, passing startled Sidhe, rushing down a white hallway, vaulted ceiling lit with glowing globes. I felt my stomach heave from the double view and turned away, keeping my attention on Thalion and my internal focus rather than trying to follow along with the others.

My connection was more immediate anyway. I felt his heart constrict, though his body showed no weakness. The door to the chamber he turned to flew open, our dual vision searching the main room. Nothing. Empty, but for lush furnishings all in white and gold and silver. He paced, slower this time, through the archway and into the bedchamber.

Again, nothing.

She isn't here, he sent.

Keep looking. I had a very bad feeling. *The real Bronagh has to be somewhere.*

Only one last place to search when her wardrobe turned up only discarded clothing. Private bath, all crystal marble and shining light. The giant pool of a tub sat full, overflowing even, pink water spilling over the white fur thrown at the bottom of the stairs.

Something lay beneath the still surface, strands of dark ribbon floating around the edges.

Thalion gasped as my power of water reached through him and prodded the surface.

Bronagh's empty emerald eyes stared up at us as she bobbed softly to the top.

Dead.

Thalion's eyes flooded with tears, shattering the vision into a prismed image. I felt myself jerked back from what he witnessed as Gram pulled on me.

We knew she had to be dead, she sent. *And now the queen knows. Hit her hard.*

She didn't have to tell me twice.

"You see what you've done," I said, cold, precise, fury turning to a sharp-edged attack. "Your own advisor dead, thanks to you. Your daughter missing. Thanks to you."

There is no soul here, Thalion sent, a wide message. I could feel him turn and come back toward us. *Bronagh's essence is gone as well.*

Whose soul is more powerful? Looking like Cian, like Fergus, would have gotten Ameline in. But if she still had him, how could she change her appearance to Bronagh?

Cian is powerful, Thalion sent, clearly following my train of thought. *But Bronagh more so. If Ameline was able to adapt to his appearance, having Bronagh's more powerful soul would make it simple to take on her features.*

261

All that sympathy. All Bronagh's help. Of course, she'd wanted Shaylee and I free of the queen. No way Ameline could steal Shaylee if Aoilainn had her thralled.

Damn her.

"Lost to you," I pushed harder, lashing at myself as much as the Seelie queen for our combined failure. "Because you wouldn't listen. Because in your arrogance you refused to pay attention, only wanting what you couldn't have."

Aoilainn stood there and took what I dished out, trembling, angry herself.

"So, Your Majesty," I ground out the address like an insult, "here's the question. Are you going to continue to ignore the fact this is your fault or are you going to step up and do something to help?"

I don't know what I expected from her. Too many years, too much time passed. Aoilainn didn't say anything. Simply turned with her army behind her and left us there.

Well, at least she wasn't planning to hinder. So that was something.

War averted, I hugged myself, anxiety for Shaylee eating away at my insides as I spun on Odhran and Niamh. "I think Ameline has already left." She'd promised me she'd bring Shaylee to the Gate, didn't she? Thanked me.

Thanked me.

Oh. My. Swearword.

"She took Shaylee with her." Shudders gripped me, a sick feeling in my stomach driving bile to the back of my throat.

Ameline had Shaylee.

Ameline had Shaylee.

Ameline had—

"I want to help you," Odhran said. "But the Gate is on the Seelie side. And while I know Aoilainn has gone home to lick her wounds, I can't imagine she will simply stand aside and let me invade her realm."

I knew that already. But I was really happy to hear he still believed me. Maybe more so now.

I caught a flash of streaking white and turned to see Thalion come to a halt next to the barrier as Odhran went on.

"I will be here," he said, "we all will be. When the time comes. You can call on us, Sydlynn. And when you do, the Unseelie will answer."

"My king." Venner fell to his knees at the Fey ruler's feet. "What of my fate?"

Niamh grinned and prodded the lordling with one black-booted toe. "We'll have to talk about that, won't we, Odhran?"

"We will," the king said, face and voice stern. When he caught my eye, he winked. "But there will be consequences."

Nice to know Venner wasn't going to get out of this

without some kind of punishment. But he had fulfilled his side of the bargain, and now that he was home, hopefully his days making a pain of himself were over.

"You'll keep an eye on him, I take it?" I could feel the pull of need to leave, leave now, but didn't want to alienate the only friends I'd made here.

"We will." Odhran obviously understood, because he gestured and made an archway for us to pass through. "Now go, and save your princess before it's too late."

I turned to run through, only to feel Venner's mind touch mine.

I owe you a debt, he sent. *And I will repay you someday.*

Whatever. I was already moving, Thalion leading the way back to the Gate, the others with me. I used all the power at my disposal to boost my speed, felt Thalion manipulating the landscape and, within moments, the Gate came into view.

Closed. Dark. But Shaylee's trail, the familiar feeling of her, led right to it. And Ameline's, too.

I stopped, fists impacting the rough wood once before I turned to Fergus. "Open it." I couldn't any more, not without Shaylee.

Fergus shook his head, eyes going to Thalion. "I cannot," he said. "The power belongs to the prince."

I spun on Thalion, watched doubt cross over his face as one hand settled on the Gate.

"Seriously," I said. "You still doubt?"

"No," he said, letting his hand drop. "But you will go and rescue her. And she will remain with you."

"You were the one who said she's different now," I said. "And you're right." I drew a breath, clenching against the possibility. "But if she decides she wants to come home, I promise you, I won't hold her back."

Thalion hesitated one more moment before nodding. "I trust your honor," he said. "I know you will not betray it."

Yeah. Not like some Sidhe I knew.

The Gate lit up, bright green, edges glowing as Thalion's power cracked the seal. It gaped wide on the other side, showing the chamber.

The very full chamber.

chapter thirty three

Mom spun on the other side, eyes wide, waving at me with urgency while a crowd of Enforcers flanked her. Three familiar old faces, pinched in fury, stared at me through the wavering bubble. The board of governors had come, probably looking for Venner. Though, as far as I was concerned, he wasn't their problem anymore. If he ever was at all.

Damned witch politics.

Looked like it was frying pan to fire time.

Bring it.

I couldn't hear Mom through the barrier, probably Thalion's doing. Or the fact she didn't have Sidhe blood.

Not that I did anymore either.

"Thank you." I turned to Thalion. "Hopefully we're not too late." Please. Please, let us not be too late.

He bowed his head to me and backed away. I caught

Gram hugging Fergus out of the corner of my eye and a spark of curiosity bloomed. I'd have to ask her about the little smile they shared as she let him go.

Later. When Shaylee was safe and Ameline was dead.

I plunged my hands into the barrier, but felt myself repelled. "I can't get through." Panic rose while my demon howled her frustration.

Gram grabbed my arm and pulled me away. "Silly girl," she said. "Like this." Her Sidhe soul parted the veil while Thalion gasped. Gram looked over her shoulder at him with a wicked smile.

"Don't try to trick my granddaughter again," she said. *If you had managed to break the seal, he could have kept your own soul here.*

The bastard. I almost aimed a kick at him, but chose to ignore him instead. So much for trusting me.

"Forgive me," he said, real sorrow on his face. "You're all I have left of her, despite your human form."

He'd be getting a piece of me, all right. Just not the one he wanted. My foot, his butt.

Look out.

Shaylee's touch vanished when Gram parted the veil, pulling me back to what was really important.

She's gone. No panic this time. Good work, Syd.

Gram shrugged. *The touch was residual at best*, she sent. *We know where Ameline went, at least. And will have an easier time tracking her on the other side without the glamour to distract us.*

Shaylee.

And the other two souls Ameline carries. Gram snorted. *That girl is nothing if not predictable when it comes to power. You think she's given up Liam or Bronagh? Not likely. I'm betting she hasn't made it far and probably has a bit of a battle on her hands now that the three of them are inside her.*

I hadn't thought of that. But it made me feel heaps better.

Mom beckoned again and this time I didn't hesitate. The soap-bubble feeling of the veil sucked at me before I popped through on the other side, staggering into my mother who caught me as I stumbled over the stone floor. The air felt different, heavier, thicker, the glamoured perfection of the Seelie kingdom fading to memory.

Quaid came through after me, Charlotte at his side. She shuddered as she returned to human shape, shaking as if she was still a wolf before crossing to stand behind me. Whatever transformation happened between there and here, her hair, once dyed black, was blonde again.

Weird.

Quaid paused next to me, drawing me against him, hugging me close. I breathed in his scent, let his magic surround me a moment before pulling away.

"Thanks for the help," I said.

"I just wish it ended better." He turned to Pender

who hovered behind Mom. "Ready to report, sir."

I watched Quaid go, the warm feeling he left me with fading as I thought of Shaylee. The gaping hole inside was closing over, filling in with my other magicks, but I knew it would never heal, not completely.

Not without her.

Before I could open my mouth to deliver my own update, Gertrude Santos shouldered Mom aside, tiny body quivering, wrinkled face pruned in anger.

"What have you done with our prisoner?" Like she'd arrested him personally or something. Or even wanted to admit when I'd told them first Venner wasn't to be trusted.

Sigh.

"He's with his king," I said. "The Unseelie ruler. Big guy. Super scary. I'd be having kittens if I was Venner." When had I learned to lie with so much sarcasm?

The news took the woman aback, one hand pressing to her creased bosom, lips forming a puckered "O" of horror. "You terrible, terrible child," she said.

"Terrible," Elegance Faster agreed, thin body towering over even the Enforcers. She made me think of the Sidhe and the Unseelie all over again.

Sad, but she'd probably fit in, no problem.

Periwinkle Rhodes bounced her round self between Mom and Gertrude, a bright pink, monogramed handkerchief waving in front of her nose, tiny glasses sliding to perch near the round ball end. "What have you done?"

Well, Mom warned me. Didn't she?

Gertrude turned and snapped her fingers at an Enforcer hovering behind Mom. "Arrest this miserable child," she growled in her gravel voice while the other two bobbed their heads.

Mom's face had settled into a stone mask. Which meant she was about to explode.

I had to salvage this somehow.

"Coven Leader," I said with a push of power behind it. That made them stare. Good.

Time to use the rules to our advantage, Gram sent with an evil chuckle. *Finally*.

She was so right. "Since he is Sidhe," I said, almost casually, "and attacked a Sidhe Gatekeeper, this is really none of your business."

I wished I had a camera. Video, preferably. Just to catch all the spluttering.

"But his association with that terror, Ameline Benoit!" Gertrude turned to her friends, clearing seeking support.

"Actually," I said in my best Mom tone while my mother's cheeks turned very pink, lips twitching from holding in what was obviously a sudden turn from anger to laughter, "as it turns out, it was only Hortense Spaft who had dealings with Ameline. And so, Venner's crimes were against the Sidhe alone. And the Sidhe are dealing with him."

Pender joined us, planting himself at Mom's side. And from the stern look on his face, he'd heard enough.

"Ladies," he said, "while the Enforcer order and the High Council appreciate your commitment to the safety of all witches, you are severely outside your jurisdiction."

More huffing. Until Elegance jabbed one of her long, skinny fingers at me. "She is a student at Coven Hall," she said with a smug smile. "That makes this a situation of interest."

"As is the Sidhe boy," Gertrude pounced on her friend's reasoning.

Were they really serious?

Mom's magic crackled at last, sending them scurrying back.

"As your Council Leader," she said in that quiet tone I knew not to push against when it was aimed at me unless I wanted a nuclear argument, "I'm siding with our Enforcer order. Ladies, return to your duties. At once."

Not even they were willing to go up against Mom head-on, I guessed, because they huffed and they puffed and they gathered themselves up before turning for the exit.

But not before Gertrude fixed me with her baleful stare.

"We're watching you, miss," she said. "See you back

271

at school, dear."

Shudder.

Mom's mind touched mine as they left. *Very quick thinking,* she sent. *But such excuses will only hold up for so long, Syd.*

I know. I shrugged. *What did you want me to do?*

Are you done badgering the girl, or are you going to hear what happened? Gram's mind reached through me to Mom's from across the barrier where she still stood with Fergus.

Mom's eyes widened when she turned to look at her mother. But she stayed quiet, so I dove in.

It took about two minutes to dump everything on Mom. I watched Galleytrot cross next while I spoke, the big dog shared a hugging goodbye from Fergus. I knew Mom listened, but grinned at the shock on her face as Gram, the young and beautiful version of her, kissed Fergus soundly before turning and sliding through the veil. It was so weird, not just watching her—me, in a way—kiss someone—Liam, really—but even more so when she emerged on our side. For the barest heartbeat, she remained as she had been, young and stunningly Sidhe before the real world resumed control and her old, familiar face with its halo of white hair and florescent-laced tennis shoes reappeared.

Gram grinned at me before turning to blow Fergus a kiss. He returned the gesture with a beaming smile that reminded me of Liam.

Another ache to heal.

Thalion stared at me as the Gate swung shut, eyes never leaving mine until the doorway closed and he and Fergus were gone.

Mom listened as I finished telling her what happened, fidgeting slightly from time to time as though wanting to ask questions, but not interrupting. When I finally wound down, she gestured to the Enforcers surrounding her.

"Fine Ameline Benoit," she snapped. "She made it past us somehow and I want to know how."

"It's possible she left here before you arrived." Gram sighed and looked down at her wrinkled hands. "Sucks getting old," she said. "Don't ever do it if you can help it."

"Not something I have to worry about," I said. Paused. Maybe I did, now.

Gram fixed me with a glare before pinching my cheek, as if knowing where my mind went. "We'll find them both," she said. "Let's get cracking."

Mom's hand on my shoulder stopped me before I could follow. "I've stretched this as far as I can," she said, pain on her face, in her voice. "In Syd's own words to the board of governors, this is Sidhe business. And Syd is no longer Sidhe."

Gram growled. "Sophistry," she snapped. "Is Liam still dying or isn't he? Is the world still at risk because of Ameline or not? Don't be a fool, Miriam. This has to end, and Syd is the only one who can draw Shaylee out of Ameline when we find her."

"Then, when we find her," Mom said, "Syd will be summoned."

Summoned. Yeah, like that was going to happen.

"Don't get in my way, Mom," I said, pulling my arm free. "If the Council wants to bitch about interference, let them. If they want to arrest me for it, fine. But I'm getting Shaylee back. And I'm taking Ameline down. With or without your help."

Mom hesitated. Slumped. "Oh, Syd," she whispered. "If only they understood how valuable you are to them. What your courage could mean for all of us." She hugged me quickly. "Liam is here. We had to take the risk and move him. I hoped the Gate's proximity would help, but he's weaker than ever."

I left her, pushing my way through the crowd of Enforcers, stopping at Liam's bedroom door.

He lay under the spreading canopy of leaves, pale and still, the twin Kennecott's still beside him. And Sashenka, holding his hand. A stab of jealousy broke through only to die away when Shenka looked up and met my eyes.

"Syd!" She left his side, coming to hug me. "You're all right." She hesitated, her magic touching mine before one hand covered her mouth, tears welling. "Shaylee?"

"Long story." I crossed to Liam, sat where she had sat, knowing I had to go, that I didn't have time for this, but unable to just leave him without a moment to check in.

"He has stabilized," Lula said without prompting. "The cavern knows him, welcomes him. But that is all."

Sidhe magic. Time was different in the realm, wasn't it? Maybe that was true here, as well. If so, it might be slowing the progress of his degeneration.

To my shock, Liam's eyes fluttered open and met mine. I never expected him to wake and, from the surprised look on the twin's faces, they hadn't either.

"Syd." He coughed softly, tried again. "Where did you go?"

Tears trickled down my cheeks as the hopelessness and frustration finally won their way out of me. "I'm sorry," I whispered, choking around my tears. "I'm trying to save you."

He smiled, a sweet, crooked smile. "Silly," he said. "You already have. Do you know how much I love you, Syd?"

My heart clenched as I reached for his hands, gripped them in mine. No magical connection linked us and yet I felt him still. In my heart. Part of me always worried the only reason I felt attracted to him and he to me was because of our shared magic. And while not a bad basis for love, there was no promise such a tie would last past the fire of that power's passion.

But as I sat there, his thin hands in mine, his fading

life still loving me, the last of my resistance burst and my heart bloomed open.

"I love you, too." I did, oh, I did, so very much. I leaned forward, pressing my lips to his forehead, his cheek, his lips. All my worry and fear for him, my terror for the loss of Shaylee, my hatred for Ameline and Aoilainn, faded in the light of his love. And mine.

He answered with the barest movement, but he answered.

"I'm sorry we don't have time," he breathed in my ear. "But if I have to die, it's happy, knowing you love me."

He had to go and shatter my heart all over again, didn't he?

Not this loss. Not now.

"Don't give up on me," I said. "Or yourself. Hear me, O'Dane? This isn't over yet."

Liam nodded ever so slightly before a racking cough tore out of his throat. The twins' magic dove on him, smothering the cough, putting him back to sleep.

"He doesn't have much time," Lula whispered. "If you're going to return his soul, you have to hurry."

I leaned away from him with a firm nod, swiping at the tears on my face. Turned to stand, to leave him, as hard as that was, harder than I thought it would be. Looked up.

Into Quaid's sad eyes.

He'd seen it. All of it. Heard it too, no question.

I need your help. It wasn't fair of me to ask.

But Quaid didn't hesitate, offering his hand. *No matter what we feel for each other, Syd, no matter what's to come, I told you I'm always here for you. And I am. Even when I screw up so badly I lose the only thing that ever really mattered to me.*

I took his offered support, let my magic reach for his. *Let's find Ameline.*

chapter thirty four

Why does it always seem to be what goes around comes back again? I left the confines of the Sidhe wards, with Gram's help, stepping out into the cool, musty air of the basement hallway. And reached for the veil while my demon sniffed out Shaylee.

She was surprisingly easy to find. Just like Gram said. And it was all because of greed. The veil parted and welcomed me, Quaid and Charlotte beside me, Galleytrot at our backs, sliding the short distance through the flexible membrane toward our target.

I leaped from the edge of the veil when it opened, power surging, rage rising as never before, almost consuming me as I prepared to confront Ameline.

She wasn't there. But the trace of her was. Outside the gaping hole of a cavern I knew well, that I'd once thought would be my death at the hands of Cesard and my vampire essence, tied to the demon trapped there. And once to save Sebastian and, through him, my mother when she stood trial.

So like Ameline to try to hide. I stomped my way past the reopened entry, past the stone Sebastian and I reset before leaving last time. I had Ameline cornered in a cavern where elemental magic was worthless.

Where Sidhe earth magic was worthless.

What was she doing?

I hate this place. Quaid shuddered as we traveled the dark, musty tunnel to the main cavern. I remembered. We'd been here once before, and almost died. He'd tried to protect me when my magic was blocked, my demon power held back by the wards, which kept the demon lord Torsh from escaping.

Me too, I sent. *Keep your eyes open.*

Maybe she chose this place because she thought it might unnerve me.

Not by a long shot. I still had a demon and a vampire to back me up. A wereguard and a hound of the Wild Hunt. And a very protective Enforcer who, powerless thanks to the element blocking wards or not, would be there when I needed him.

Ameline better watch the hell *out*.

I fumbled my way along in the perma light as my demon adjusted my vision, the large cavern looming ahead. She was ready for anything, as was my vampire,

279

tense and crackling with magic.

Anything but what we found.

Ameline had fallen to her knees in the center of the cavern at some point, but didn't make it back to her feet. She clutched at her stomach while her body rippled with green fire. Expecting a trick, I threw up a wall of demon magic as a shield while I let my vampire sniff her out.

Ameline looked up, eyes flaring green, face contorting as her features twisted from face to face to face.

Liam.

Bronagh.

Shaylee.

They fought her, all of them, twining together, driving her to gag and moan, tipping her over onto her side, blood leaking from her nose.

Caught by her own greed. Just like Gram said.

Perfect.

Quaid eased forward, looking around as he did. I hadn't considered she might have backup. Silly of me, really. She hadn't hesitated to use others in the past. But no, she was alone.

Just her and three very angry Sidhe souls.

"Let them go, Ameline." I crossed to her slowly, standing over her, my shields firmly in place just in case it was some kind of trick. That I would never put past her.

She shuddered, let out a whimper. "No, I need them." She writhed on the stone floor, reaching for my foot, crying out when her hand hit my shield and was repelled with amber fire. "Help me!"

I laughed. Out loud. Doubled over from it. Choked on it.

"You've got to be kidding me." The urge to slam her into the ground with as much power as I could muster was so strong it was only my vampire's firm hold on me that kept me from turning Ameline into a multi-colored smear on the ground. "You are really. Freaking. Kidding. Me."

She sobbed once, rolled over, rocking as she clutched herself, more blood leaking from her nose, from her right eye, sliding from her ear to pool on the ground.

"All of this." My power bunched, ready to slice and dice. "Liam, Venner, all of it. Just to steal Shaylee from me."

"She would never leave on her own," Ameline whispered. Coughed. "I had no choice." She shuddered then, moaning before falling still. "You must help me," she said. "I'm dying." "Good," I said, absolutely without sympathy. "Hurry up and get it over with. I have stuff to do."

Ameline's lip curled. "You fool," she groaned. "Don't you understand who we are to each other? We will be allies in the fight to come."

"Never." I poked her with the toe of my sneaker. "Are you not done dying yet? Really, you can't do anything right."

Ameline coughed, spraying blood against my shield. The droplets burned up without touching me. I shuddered. So. Gross.

"You should have learned your lesson with Todd." The demon boy whose soul she stole the last time she tried this ridiculousness hadn't wanted her to control him, either.

"I had to try." She choked on more blood, spitting it up. "I need them to be maji. You know that. All must be equal, in balance, or the transformation can't be completed." News to me. Nice of Iepa, my maji connection, to share that bit of info, though I figured she hadn't had to bother. What Ameline fought for, tooth and nail, had come naturally to me.

If what Ameline said was even true.

Something to be said for this fate stuff, I guess.

Ameline's eyes narrowed, and even in her pain her vindictive spirit showed. "You're not maji anymore either, are you?"

Before I could respond, Shaylee's face took over, her fury rippling over Ameline's body while the tortured girl screamed.

"Syd." Quaid's low voice caught my attention. "We need to take her into custody now."

"No," I said. "We need to wait. Just a few more minutes." I looked down at the dying girl. "That should do it, right, Ameline?"

Syd. Quaid's mental voice wouldn't let me ignore him. *Listen to me. You've never killed anyone. Or let them die. It's a huge thing. You have to trust me on that.*

Like I cared. *Back off, Quaid.*

I won't. His mental voice was weak, but he clung to me anyway, despite his muted power. *You're not this person, Syd. Let her go to trial. Let them burn her at the stake for her crimes. There is a more important job for you to do right now.*

Liam. He was right. And yet... just a few more minutes and I'd never have to worry about Ameline again.

Fine. I pulled away from Quaid. *But I'm taking the others before you bring her in.*

Agreed. Quaid joined me while Charlotte hovered.

I reached for Shaylee, my demon and my vampire calling to her, the echo of the family magic reaching out. And she came, in a surge of power, flooding me, linking with me, sobbing her joy, pouring into me so fast I rocked on my heels and hand to clutch at Quaid to stay upright.

Ameline gasped, a moment of relief turning to more agony as the other two souls, clearly understanding their release was nigh, redoubled their efforts.

Syd, Syd, Syd, Syd! Shaylee hugged me, clasped me close, her power filling the empty space as I sobbed and welcomed her home, my other magicks doing the same. It was as if she'd never left, her earth magic flooding me with power, not dampened by the elemental controls of the cavern.

I am Sidhe, she sent. *These wards can't contain me.*

Ameline's mistake. She must have thought the cavern would give her the breathing room to figure out what to do.

I loved it when a bad guy's plan went to hell in a hand basket.

I turned to Galleytrot, my hope, at last, alive and well. "Go tell Mom we found her," I said. "To send Enforcers. We're bringing Liam's soul back."

Galleytrot chuffed and spun, racing off without a moment of hesitation.

I turned back, refocused on Ameline and her struggles. *We can't hold the others*, Shaylee sent when I tried to reach for Liam. *But there are two here who can carry them if they are willing?*

I glanced sideways at Quaid. *Shaylee says you'll have to carry one of the souls. And Charlotte the other. Can you handle that?*

He nodded, gritting his teeth. *You're going to give me Liam's aren't you?*

I almost laughed. Almost. *It's either that or a girl.*

He grunted. *Give me fairy boy*, he sent. *And hurry up about it.*

chapter thirty five

I resealed the entrance to the cave again before turning to watch the six Enforcers, led by leader Pender Tremere himself, bundle up the still weak and hurting Ameline in their grasp and whisk her off to prison.

It wasn't until they finally disappeared, the witch girl firmly wrapped in Enforcer magic, her eyes never leaving mine with that old, cold smile on her face, that I actually let out the breath I'd been holding.

So sure something would go wrong. Any second now.

But I had other things to think about. Charlotte shuddered a few times, her wolf emerging in her eyes as she struggled to settle the Sidhe soul inside her. While Bronagh's spirit had gone to the weregirl willingly, it was clear the two weren't really happy with the situation.

Quaid simply stared at me, in a bit of a daze, though when I reached for his hand, his magic slid over my skin, love tied to Liam's.

Freaky weird.

I tore open the veil and pulled them along with me, slipping through the welcoming edge of the barrier, feeling my demon grandmother's soul, trapped in the Node, whisper welcome. She and I hadn't been the best of buddies or anything and as much as I wished she was still alive so Dad didn't have to be Ruler of Demonicon, I kind of liked her better now.

Death became her. Tragic, yeah?

The Gate wards parted easily for me as I crossed from the library basement and into the cavern. Usually, I worried a little Liam or I might catch trouble from the maintenance guy who kept town hall and the old archive going, and that was just two of us. Adding Charlotte, Galleytrot and a whole heap of Enforcers, not to mention the healer twins, Mom, and Gram meant a big chunk of magic went toward keeping the normals who worked here out of the know.

Not that it was hard, to be honest. All these years living with the Gate and its subtle pressure to ignore anything unusual did part of the job for us. Still, Mom had her hands full.

Not my problem. I steered Quaid into Liam's room and to his side while Mom and Gram rushed forward from the Gate where they talked with a group of Enforcers. The twins looked up, hope on their faces as

Quaid sat down next to the young Gatekeeper and took his hand. Awkwardly. With a grimace.

"Now what?" He looked up, chocolate eyes meeting mine.

Shaylee had the answer. She embraced Quaid with her energy, reached for Liam, already eager to go, and created a bridge between the two. Liam's lost soul, the Seelie Cian, gushed from Quaid in a torrential river of green magic, slamming into Liam's wasted body so hard my Sidhe friend gasped. Sighed. Opened his eyes.

Smiled up at me as his face filled out, skin flushing with color, the spark of green back in his hazel eyes. His power, that of the soul he carried, reached out for me and hugged me close.

Thank you, my love, he whispered.

Teary, me? Naw.

Quaid left me there and, though I wanted to follow him, talk to him, make things right between us after the choice I'd made, Liam took priority. I'd chosen him, hadn't I? And I needed to be sure he was going to be okay.

In a few short minutes he looked so much better I thought he might try to get up.

"Not just yet," Phon laughed. Lula stroked Liam's forehead, making his eyes droop.

His mind, still solidly connected with mine, fought sleep. *I felt his love for you*, Liam sent. *While he carried Cian.*

Syd, are you sure?

I bent and kissed his lips, sparks of Sidhe fire passing between us. Liam breathed me in, hands strong again gripping my face as he opened his heart completely and welcomed me inside.

Silly question.

He fell asleep with a smile on his lips.

I'd celebrate later. One last task to complete first. And it weighed on me yet.

Mom hugged me, Gram too, both silent as I passed through the door and headed for the Gate. A touch and a call to it sent flashes of green fire along the edges. It swung open, almost happily, as though welcoming so much activity, probably the most it had seen since it was created. I stood there, a firm hold on my heart as the door gaped wide.

Thalion stood waiting in the same spot I'd left him, as if rooted in that place. And beside him, her face a composed mask, was Aoilainn. Shaylee hissed softly at the sight of her mother while Charlotte twitched once.

This is your chance. I spoke directly to the Sidhe princess inside me. *You could have your life back, if limited. Though I'm sure there's a way to make your new body stronger.*

Sydlynn, she sent, hugging me, drawing all of my magicks to her. *This is where I belong.*

"Mother," Shaylee spoke up. "Thalion. I understand Sydlynn promised to give me a chance at my freedom. To return to you. If I so chose."

Neither spoke. Shaylee's magic cracked like a whip, sending a flare over the barrier between planes.

"I will never leave her," Shaylee said, voice vibrating with power. "We have a job to do together, a greater destiny. And I will not fail her or the fate in store because of some selfish queen and her need to control her daughter." She met Thalion's eyes. "Or a spoiled prince who pouts over being denied."

Careful, I sent to her, wincing a little. *We might need them eventually.*

No, Shaylee sent. *They will need us.*

Okay then.

Aoilainn turned and left without a word, passing from view in a moment. But Thalion lingered, his magic touching the barrier, reaching for us. Charlotte stepped forward, one hand touching the surface of the bubble. With a soft growl from her and a musical sigh from the Sidhe soul she carried, Bronagh oozed out of the weregirl and slid through the veil. She formed for a moment on the other side, a thin column of green before flashing into intense light and vanishing.

"We will care for her," Thalion said. "And, if she chooses, find a host on your plane to whom she can be reborn."

I hadn't known the real Bronagh, but Shaylee's contentment with his words was enough for me.

"She might not see it," Thalion said as he stepped back from the veil, "but I understand. I will watch, and continue to confer with Odhran and Niamh of the Unseelie. And I will be waiting when you call for me."

With that, Thalion bowed his head, flowing silver hair falling forward to mask his face as the Gate sighed and groaned and finally closed.

chapter thirty six

I didn't go back to Harvard right away. The Kennecott twins wanted to watch over Liam in the cavern for a few days. And I needed to stay near him.

When I finally went home to my house, collapsed on my own bed, the quiet night outside soothing me close to sleep, I was thankful for the break. Shenka returned to school, promising to catch me up on work if it killed her. I wasn't worried, not really.

If I failed Elemental Interactions, it wouldn't be the end of the world.

Snort.

When I felt him in the back yard, tears welled in my eyes, but my body was already moving, carrying me down the stairs and to the door. I sat next to him in the chill September night, my hip tucked against his on the bench, so familiar, this meeting place, it almost felt like it would never end.

But everything ends. Everything. Eventually.

Quaid slid his arm around my shoulders and I settled against him, though without romantic intent. Just a comfortable, calm and soothing moment, two friends supporting each other. Sharing the stillness without needing a thing.

Until he spoke.

"I felt his love for you." His deep voice rumbled from his chest, leather jacket creaking as he shifted just a fraction. I turned to look up at him, to feel the warmth of his breath on my face as he met my eyes.

"He said the same thing." I touched the stubble on Quaid's cheek with my fingertips, the chase of magic racing through me and to my toes. My demon hummed her discontent, but sadly pulled back as I let my hand drop.

Quaid nodded, jaw working.

"Thank you," I said. "For being there for me. When I really needed you."

He shrugged. "I seemed to be more of a hindrance than a help," he said.

"Not this time. You have no idea." I leaned my head against his shoulder. "It means a lot to me, Quaid. To know I'm not alone."

My magicks hugged me gently. Never alone.

"You know I love you," he said. "And every day I

struggle with the choice I made."

"I know," I whispered. "But Quaid, no matter how much we want to hold on to each other, there's comes a time when we have to admit it's done." I couldn't believe I said it. That I was so calm about it. Would probably sob my heart out later. But, for now, I meant every word.

And he knew it, from the way his magic retreated from me, his body tensing. He didn't pull away physically, still cradling me against him, but the last of the magic that held us together was broken.

"What I felt in him... he really loves you." He sounded like he just admitted that truth to himself. "And he'll take good care of you. So I don't have to worry."

I laughed. "Like I need someone to take care of me."

Quaid kissed my temple. "Syd," he said. "Someone has to."

"All I ever wanted was for you to be there," I said. "And you were, this time. But I need someone who always will be."

Quaid stood, pulled me up beside him, hugged me to his broad chest while his heart beat against mine before letting me go for the last time and stepping away.

"Be happy, Sydlynn Hayle," he said.

I sat there a long time after he was gone, trying to decide if the ache in my chest was real or just regret.

Regardless, Quaid and I, after all we'd been through, were finally done.

chapter thirty seven

School. Wow. My dorm room felt like an alien planet. But Shenka's smiling face and an eager hug greeted me when I finally returned, so that made all the difference.

She immediately began to grill me, dragging me down to sit on her bed beside her. "How's Liam?"

"He's completely fine," I said, tucking one leg under me. "The healers said he's made a full recovery." And from what I could tell, from what Shaylee felt, that was true. I still worried, especially now I'd decided I was going to throw caution to the wind when it came to him.

When, I still hadn't settled on. I wanted to make sure he was back and life was even a little normal before trying the relationship thing.

Shenka smiled and squeezed my hand. "I'm so happy for you two," she said. "You know Tippy's going to be all kinds of jealous?"

Let her. "Oh well," I said. "She's got lots of prospects."

Shenka laughed. "Tell me about it."

"Thank you, by the way." I hugged her impulsively. Her scent always reminded me of her home in California and the ocean. "For taking care of Liam."

She leaned back with a big smile, white teeth flashing against her lovely dark skin. "What's a second for?"

Okay, that floored me. "Seriously?"

She nodded, fast and jerky. "If you still want me?"

I didn't get to shriek and hug her again in excitement. Not because I didn't want to, but because the door to our room was knocked upon quite firmly, twice, before it swung open to bang with some force against the far wall.

I stood, my magic surging around me in protective mode, Shaylee snarling. She'd acquired a certain level of bravery since I'd reabsorbed her into myself and her reaction made me proud.

Not that my pride would do much against the shaking and clearly angry Tallah Hensley who stood just over the threshold, glaring at me. A flicker of motion over her shoulder drew my eyes, Mom nodding slowly to me as I turned my attention back to the leader of the Hensley coven.

Shenka's sister ground her jaw a moment before she spoke. "I understand you're trying to poach my second, Coven Leader Hayle."

That was hardly fair. "Your second volunteered," I said, going cold. I liked Tallah, but no way was she pushing me around.

Tallah's eyes narrowed as she turned to Shenka. I glanced at my friend, saw how pale she'd gone, an ashen tone to her dark skin. But Sashenka held her ground under the pressure of her sister's magic.

More pride. Hell yeah.

"Is that true?"

I wanted to protest. No coven leader should use their magic to coerce one of their family to stay. Mom's quick headshake told me to stay out of it.

Trust her, Gram sent in a thin thread. Of course she was paying attention. Nosy old—

At least one of us is, she grunted. *Watch*.

Shenka's shoulders went back, unbowed, her chin rising. "It is, Coven Leader Hensley," she said. "I've considered for quite some time it's not a good idea for me to be your second. That you, and our coven, need someone you can lean on, consider an ally. Not a little sister who you think needs protecting." She turned to me. "I approached Syd about being her second. Not the other way around. I have you to thank for the skills I've learned." Her tone softened as her magic reached back for Tallah. "I am an excellent second. But I can't do my job effectively if I'm always considered to be someone you can't take seriously."

Tallah's face crumbled, her magic retreating. "I don't do that, do I?"

Shenka's smile was impish. "Sometimes. Tal, I need to fly. And so do you, sis."

What was I doing? I'd struggled with this before. Tallah was my friend, Shenka, too. How could I break up their family? But the quiet moment the sisters spent, finally smiling at each other, their magic now warm and kindly, told me Shenka had done what she felt was right.

As long as it didn't mean hard feelings between Tallah and I. But if it did? So be it.

Tallah glanced at me, her smile fading. "Take care of her," she said. "Or else."

"I intend to," I said. "Though I have a feeling she'll be taking care of me more often than not."

Tallah coughed out a laugh. Rolled her eyes. "Fine, you pair. You're a good match." Tallah turned to Mom. "I approve the release of my sister to the Hayle coven."

More damned politics. Mom smiled and nodded. "I'm happy to witness."

Tallah hesitated before crossing to her sister and hugging her. "I love you. Don't be a stranger." A tear tracked down Tallah's face before she sniffled and stepped away. Taking the Hensley family magic with her.

Shenka shuddered as the blue power flowed out of her, snapping off at her fingertips as she dropped her hands.

Hurry up, girl, Gram sent, breaking me out of watching mode and into action. *Don't make the poor child wait.*

Oh. Crap. Right. I reached out to Shenka with the power of the Hayle coven, feeling it welcome her, gliding around her, sliding inside and settling where the Hensley magic had once sat. She smiled at me as I grinned like an idiot.

"Welcome to the family," I said. "Second Hensley."

Shenka hugged me, laughing as our power connected along the bonds of the coven, spreading out to the rest of the family who embraced her with magic as I did with my arms.

Finally, Gram sent. *Took you long enough.*

Smartass grandmother.

chapter thirty eight

Well, hello there life. Back to quiet, are we?

We'd just see about that.

I wasn't all that shocked to learn Hortense Spaft escaped custody. But with Ameline still firmly in the clink, I didn't really care what the tall, scary Unseelie woman was up to.

Not while Ameline sent me almost constant messages, asking to see me in person. I refused to read them after a while, accept them at all shortly after that. The poor court pages had their hands full and though one of my scowls sent them scurrying when they continued to try to deliver, Ameline didn't quit.

You'd think I'd be feeling all heroic and confident now that Ameline was behind bars and magic. I just couldn't muster much past nervous anxiety.

Let her rot in her cell until they burned her alive. I'd

be happy to watch.

So much for Quaid and his worry about me and death. He had no idea what I was capable of.

I was a little disappointed Mom decided to pardon Sonja O'Dane, though. I knew she felt sorry for the woman, but having Liam's mother hanging around all the time, doting on him and insisting she spend as much of his free moments alone with him as possible put a definite damper on any attempt we made to see where our mutual love was going.

I started to despise her, honestly. And from the long-suffering looks I caught from Liam, I wasn't the only one annoyed with the whole thing.

I found I was tired of being alone, carrying the burden by myself. Having Shenka next to me, firmly ensconced as my second, really brought that truth home. Almost losing Liam taught me how much I loved him, my immortality be damned. I was ready to have a steady relationship with someone who could give me all of his attention.

Guess I just couldn't catch a break.

At least my free time away from Liam gave me the opportunity to start checking into the Brotherhood. I'd been very lax in the duties Iepa set me. I also dove into learning to understand my maji power, with help. Quaid's, of all people. I liked that it kept us close, friends. I missed him still, in my heart. But at least this way we maintained a relationship. Even if it was only about work.

I was feeling a bit put out by the lack of communication I had with my vampire family, though. I wanted their input on the Brotherhood issue, but any attempt I made to talk to Sunny, Uncle Frank or Sebastian was met with quiet. I nervously mentioned it to Mom, only to have her tell me Sunny and Uncle Frank were very busy with their new clan and Sebastian was likely doing the same.

Still. They could at least check back to say hello once in a while.

Shenka was fitting into the coven just fine. More than fine, really. Even though we were still at school through the week, she took the time every day to contact the family as individuals for little chats. And, on her insistence, though she didn't have to twist my arm, we went home to Wilding Springs every weekend for face-to-face contact.

Oddly, the Lawrence twins, Estelle and Esther, adored her. I wasn't sure why I found that weird, but I did. Maybe it had to do with the fact Shenka wasn't a Hayle until I made her one. The former Purity witches treated her with respect and I even caught them giggling with her once.

Almost died of shock.

The Happerns, our stray demon family, also welcomed her, and she them, insisting they become more involved in coven activities. I just stood back and let her do her job, silently thankful it was hers and not mine.

I sucked at bringing people together. Need a little destruction and mayhem? I'm your girl. But don't ask me to chat over sandwiches and tea.

Shenka was the perfect second.

She was right about Tippy's initial reaction to the fact Shenka had the second job. But after about an hour of sulking, she shrugged and asked to join the family anyway. It took her a little longer to get over the whole Liam thing. But even that didn't faze her.

So I considered it. Looked around at the young witches I hung out with and thought seriously about adding some fresh blood to the family. The idea of a recruitment program crossed my mind, I have to admit, starting with the Kennecott healer twins.

Why did the idea seem to make Mom so nervous?

The second Sassafras returned from Demonicon, he reached for me and firmly scolded me about going to the Sidhe realm before demanding I come get him and bring him to Harvard so he could trounce me in person. A quick trip on the veil had him in my arms while he purred and hugged me back.

I was happy to hear the transfer of power on Demonicon went more smoothly with my grandfather, Dad's father, beside him in Second Seat. Sassafras admitted it was more because Henemordonin was willing to kick butt behind the scenes to keep everyone in line than Dad's leadership skills. As a good Second Seat should. Reminded me of Shenka, only she was making friends, not bashing enemies.

While Sass congratulated me on my choice of seconds, I wondered if Dad was really the right Ruler for the job at all.

Shaylee had happily settled back inside me, but her aggressiveness wasn't easing off. I found it rather amusing, actually, and caught myself laughing at some of her more choice suggestions when Ameline's notes arrived. Tried to arrive.

I think Aoilainn created a monster.

One thing we agreed on, Venner still wasn't to be trusted, even if he said he owed me a debt. But Shaylee's attitude toward the Unseelie king and queen had shifted from horror and disgust to thoughtful contemplation. Nice to see her shedding her old cultural biases.

Considering I figured we'd need Odhran and Niamh's help in the future, that was a very good thing.

If I thought Galleytrot was protective of Liam before, I had another hound of the Wild Hunt coming. Despite the fact he was supposed to be guarding the Gate, I caught him, time and again, lurking in the darkness around campus. When I asked him how he was traveling, he refused to answer. I could only guess Mom was helping him out.

No. Not Mom. Gram. He finally confessed when he was at Harvard watching Liam, she was happily curled up on one of the fancy chairs in the archive of the Gate cavern, Rionach, her Sidhe soul, content to read and rest in the comfort of the Sidhe chamber.

According to Gram, the storm we'd seen in the Sidhe realm was still building, so I wondered if Ameline had anything to do with its creation after all. Or if the reasons behind it were far more sinister, the Brotherhood its cause as I'd suspected.

Funny how Gram knew about the storm. Her excuses about wanting to spend time in the archive, sending Galleytrot along with a big smile, might have made me nervous if I didn't trust her to protect the Gate. I fully suspected she and Fergus, still with his fragment of Cian's soul able to access the Gate, had their little visits.

I just never wanted to walk in on them. I loved Gram, but wow. TMI.

Despite the unhappiness of the board of governors trio at my outright rebellion concerning Ameline, no one came to arrest me. So I counted it a win and moved on, though I knew I had to be careful from now on. No way was I ending up in a cell matching Ameline's.

That would just make her day.

And school? Really? Really. Seemed like every time the world threatened to implode, I had school to worry about after it was all over. Oh well. Maybe it wasn't such a bad thing after all.

Quiet and boredom would tide me over.

Until everything went to hell again.

Like what you read? Find out more at
pattilarsen.com

Here's a look at the first chapter of
Book Fifteen of the Hayle Coven Novels

ANCIENT WAYS

chapter one

Sweat stung my eyes, the thud of my hands against the heavy bag vibrating up my arms and into my chest. I leaned back and lashed out with one foot in a roundhouse, connecting solidly with the cracked vinyl, the chain creaking as I sent the bag swinging.

"Nice hit." I turned, wiping my face on the shoulder of my t-shirt to the grinning face of my kick-boxing instructor. Sage steadied the bag, deep green eyes smiling as much as his mouth.

A rather yummy mouth, as it turned out. Nice little chin-cleft, too, a bit of beard shadow roughing up his wide jaw, dark brows framing that sea-colored gaze. Thick lashes framed his eyes, lashes I was jealous of the moment I walked into the gym and he looked up to greet me.

With that same smile he gave me now.

"I'm feeling more balanced." I drew a deep breath, bobbed up and down on my toes as I faced off with the bag again. "That tip you gave me about staying lower really helped."

He shrugged, his tanned skin rippling under his black tank with "Arno's Gym" straining across the front over his very nicely developed pecs. "Anything I can do to help," he said in his tenor voice. Mellow, soft for such a big guy. Sage stood almost as tall as Liam, though he had more of Quaid's bulk.

Yup, comparing boys. Fun stuff.

The only difference, this boy was normal. Completely. Not a trace of latent power to be felt. As Sage steadied the bag for me, one big shoulder holding it firm, his large hands gripping the sides for leverage, I found myself grinning.

Nothing wrong with normal now and then.

I felt my mood shift as my mind went to Liam and my decision to choose him, to see what we could do about the relationship he claimed he desperately wanted. Two thuds with my gloved fists released some of my returning tension.

Guess he didn't want to be with me as much as he said. If he did, we wouldn't have spent the last eight months with the elephant in the room that was his mother firmly placed between us, her false smile and need to be part of every single thing her son did driving me to contemplate murder.

Thud. Thud.

It felt good to let my anger out in a way that made me stronger instead of driving me to dismember and dispose of someone. Someone with salon perfect hair and the most grasping sense of ownership on the boy she'd given birth to and then served up to her Unseelie lordling master I'd ever had the misfortune to encounter.

Bitter, me? Naw.

Thud. Thud. Whack.

I caught a glimpse of Charlotte watching, standing in the corner with her arms crossed over her chest, glaring at Sage. All pissed off and wolf fur ruffled I'd decided to learn to fight.

When I told her my plans to find a gym when we came home to Wilding Springs a few weeks ago, she frowned.

"Why?" That was Charlotte. My bodywere was nothing if not blunt and to the point.

"I want to learn to defend myself," I said. She should be all for it, shouldn't she? Less worry for her. And for me.

Instead, she grunted. "That's what you have me for," she said, sounding hurt.

Seriously?

Ever since my little jaunt to the Sidhe realm, when I'd been forced to allow Shaylee and my demon to fight for me against the thralled Quaid, I'd realized just how vulnerable I was when I didn't have access to magic. Yes, I could run. So what? Anyone could do that. But, there were times when running wouldn't be an option.

Had happened now more times than I could count. Learning to fight instead, to have as much confidence in my body's ability to defend me as my magic, was at the top of my to-do list.

Right up there with finding some way to get rid of Sonja O'Dane permanently. Hopefully without turning Liam against me.

I tried to explain it to Charlotte who continued to scowl and play the deeply wounded bodywere.

Followed me to the gym I found in the phone book, still scowling.

Walked in with me, glaring.

She came with me, every time. Refused to help. To participate, despite the fact I knew what an amazing fighter she was. Could have learned a lot from her if she wasn't so damned stubborn about it. I felt terrible for the other people at the various gyms I tried who gave her a berth so wide she practically emptied every place when she walked in. It wasn't fair to the normals, not even a little. But I also knew better than to ask her to leave.

Three gyms later, the management at each spot took care of my wince-worthy worries for me by just asking us to leave. I was beginning to wonder if Charlotte would prevent me from finding the right place and if I'd have to be more firm about her staying home.

But when Sage smiled at me despite Charlotte's deadly emanations the first morning we met, standing to his full height with the biggest kettle bells I'd ever seen casually held in his very capable hands, I knew I'd found the place I was looking for. A little rough around the edges, full of bulky guys too busy looking at themselves to care what I did. Quiet. Dark.

Perfect.

"Good job, Syd," Sage said, bringing me back to the present. "Now double jab, uppercut, snap kick."

He'd taken one look at me that first day and seemed to know exactly what I needed.

"This isn't a normal gym," he said. "But you know that, right?"

I nodded, feeling a little intimidated as he towered over me, though more so by the instant zing of attraction I felt. Just what I needed, another boy to wrangle. But Sage's casual manner put me at ease as he set down the bells and offered his hand.

"Sage America," he said. Rolled his eyes in good humor. "Sad, right? My parents were latent blooming hippies who thought it would be cool to curse their son for life."

I laughed and shook his hand. "Sydlynn Hayle," I said. "Same problem."

Instant friend.

Had to love it.

From that moment on, Sage was my go-to guy, though never in a forceful or bossy way. He let me try to figure stuff out on my own, fumbling with my hand wraps, my gloves, how to handle the heavy bag at the back of the room. Each time he gave me just enough space to feel frustrated before offering a hand, a simple explanation. Made me feel like I was valuable, important to him. His hands felt warm when he pulled the wraps tight. Confident when he laced up my small boxing gloves. Totally professional when he showed me how to keep the bag from taking me out instead of the other way around. Helped me find my rhythm, made sure I was comfortable.

Left me alone as if knowing that was what I really wanted.

Then showed me how it was supposed to be done when I hesitated.

I put the attention off to the fact it was his job and he was very good at it, but still, I looked forward to seeing him every morning.

Charlotte's sudden soft growl behind me caught my attention and I turned around.

"She'll be here soon," she said, her flat, unfriendly gaze locked on Sage.

He just grinned as she backed off, returning to her

place.

"Only two kind of people need a bodyguard," Sage said, casual and quiet. "I'm guessing you're not famous."

"Infamous," I said. "But nope."

He nodded. "Rich, then. Good for you." Like it was no big deal. I could really go for this guy—

Syd. Down girl.

"So I'll see you in the morning." He released the bag, gave me a salute. "Unless you're not busy tonight."

Whoa. That came out of left field. So much for professional. Still, he said it in such an offhand way, like it didn't matter, was just an offer.

And not unwelcome.

Because yeah, I did need another boy to worry about.

Was that real regret stirring, knowing I had to turn him down? The "she" Charlotte mentioned had to take priority.

"Can't tonight," I said. "But some other night, you bet."

Tell me I didn't just agree to go out with a normal.

Sage's little grin dimpled one stubbled cheek as he turned away. "That'll be great. I'm fairly new to town, just trying to settle in. It would be nice to have someone to hang around with."

Would it ever.

"See you, Syd." Sage tipped his chin at Charlotte with another smile before leaving me to clean up and go home.

Eyes front, girl. No staring at the wide shoulders walking in the other direction tapering down to a narrow waist over hips just visible at the hem of his loose shorts, the way the black fabric cupped his rock-hard ass—

I was going to girlfriend hell.

And I was okay with it.

αδουτ τηε αυτηορ

Everything you need to know about me is in this one statement: I've wanted to be a writer since I was a little girl, and now I'm doing it. How cool is that, being able to follow your dream and make it reality? I've tried everything from university to college, graduating the second with a journalism diploma (I sucked at telling real stories), am part of an all-girl improv troupe (if you've never tried it, I highly recommend making things up as you go along as often as possible). I've even been in a Celtic girl band (some of our stuff is on YouTube!) and was an independent film maker. My life has been one creative thing after another—all leading me here, to writing books for a living.

Now with multiple series in happy publication, I live on beautiful and magical Prince Edward Island (I know you've heard of Anne of Green Gables) with my very patient husband and multitude of pets.

I love-love-love hearing from you! You can reach me (and I promise I'll message back) at patti@pattilarsen.com. And if you're eager for your next dose of Patti Larsen books (usually about one release a month) come join my mailing list! All the best up and coming, giveaways, contests and, of course, my observations on the world (aren't you just dying to know what I think about everything?) all in one place: http://smarturl.it/PattiLarsenEmail.

Last—but not least!—I hope you enjoyed what you read! Your happiness is my happiness. And I'd love to hear just what you thought. A review where you found this book would mean the world to me—reviews feed writers more than you will ever know. So, loved it (or not so much), **your honest review would make my day**. Thank you!